SO YABANG

SO YABANG

*a Filipino retelling of
a classic romance*

ZARA IRIGO

Zara Irigo Publishing

Contents

I

Bago

"Nabalitaan mo na ba, Rene?" my mom asked at the break-fast table. "May maglilipat-bahay na daw doon sa bakanteng compound sa tapat ng plaza. Kinwento sa'kin ni Mrs. Casal."

My dad barely raised his eyes from the newspaper and just mumbled something short and incoherent.

Mom's forehead creased in irritable disbelief. "Hindi mo ba itatanong kung sino?"

Dad gulped down some of his coffee before glancing up. "Sasabihin mo lang din naman sa'kin, bakit ko pa itatanong?" he pointed out before gesturing towards my older sister who was sitting to his right. "Paabot naman ng creamer, Weena."

Ate Roweena shot me a knowing look across the table as she handed Dad the plastic Coffeemate tub before going back to fixing the hair of our *bunso* sister Bingka, who was oblivious to the discussion and was simply happily eating at the table.

Eto nanaman sila, I thought with a smirk.

It was seldom in a day when my mom and dad did not argue over petty things. I figured it was possibly just the combination of age, having been married for twenty-six years, and the trials and tribulations involved with raising four children.

Or perhaps it was just that Mom and Dad's personalities had never matched to begin with—something to which Mom often attested.

My mom, Adelina Aldevinco, was from one of those Filipino families who were better off in the '50s and had fallen on hard times. She always yearned for the finer things in life and was perpetually frustrated that reality would never match her expectations.

My dad, Rene Benitez, hailed from a simple working-class family from Nueva Ecija. He worked hard to provide for the family with a taxi commission at his cousin Tito Boy's taxi company, but money wasn't always easy to come by.

Regardless, after all the years of marriage, Mom and Dad had somehow managed to tolerate and even sometimes appreciate each other's quirks.

"Magiging kapitbahay natin sila," Mom was going on with her story. "Dapat kaibiganin natin sila. Lalo na ang pamilyang 'yan," she went on, requiring no urging. "Sila Ortega. 'Yun bang mga may-ari ng New World Foods sa BTI tower sa Makati. O ngayon, kilala mo na siguro sila, diba?"

"Sige na, Adel," Dad feigned resignation. "Sila na ang pinaka-sikat na pamilya sa mundo. Mag-alay tayo ng itlog sa Linggo," he stated, turning to give his daughters a sly wink.

I met Ate Roweena's gaze again and we both chuckled.

"O, tara na, mga anak. Ma-le-late na tayo," Dad said then, standing up.

Mom just frowned at us all in disapproval but said nothing more as she helped everyone get ready for the day.

"Bingka, yung baon mo." Ate Roweena handed her an aged pink *Barbie* lunchbox. It was a hand-me-down from me, which given how old it was, had been kept in surprisingly good condition.

Bingka was eight years younger than our brother, the *unico hijo* Martin, which was to say, Bingka was a surprise baby. Her given name was Charmaine but everyone called her "Bingka", named for her favorite food.

Dad, Ate Roweena, and Bingka exited the house and loaded the taxi. We had one of those typical Filipino taxis. A white Corolla with all our names stenciled across the back trunk.

** Roweena * Carmina * Martin * Charmaine **

Much like every day, first, Bingka would be dropped off at elementary school, Ate Roweena at her office in Ortigas where she worked for an NGO before Dad would go on his daily route.

Once everyone had gone, Mom turned her attention to me with that "expectant Pinoy mom" tone.

"Ikaw Carmina," she called out. "Bakit kasi hindi ka maghanap ng matinong trabaho tulad ng Ate Rowena mo? Kaysa puro ka gitara at banda, wala namang patutunguhan 'yan. Hindi naman kayo sumasali sa 'Pinoy Idol'. Sino bang manonood sa inyo?"

I rolled my eyes as I finished clearing the table, wiping the 70's vinyl/plastic tablecloth before tossing some bread scraps to the floor for our dog Basti, an *askal*-Siberian husky mix.

Obviously, it wasn't the first time that my mom indicated her disappointment with my chosen preoccupation, claiming that my having graduated with a Sociology degree from college was just a waste of money since I was always in between jobs.

It was always either I didn't last long at a job or that time that I was in a dead-end BPO desk job in Taguig for over a year until I eventually quit.

But music had always been my first passion and I would have taken it up in college if Mom hadn't said that *that* would have been the waste of money.

I played bass guitar in our band. We were by no means famous, of course, and so far in our six years, we'd only played gigs at small local bars, but it stood to reason that that was how everyone always started out.

"Tutugtog po kami sa pista this weekend, diba nga, Mommy? Sinabi ko sa inyo 'yun," I reminded my mom.

Mom droned on, muttering as though not even hearing me. "Palibhasa kasi paborito ka ng tatay mo, kaya ayan, hinahayaan ka na lang parati, maski ano pa'ng sabihin ko. Hala sige, ewan ko ba bakit pa'ko nagsasalita. Wala namang nakikinig—"

At that moment, Martin shuffled down the hall, only passing through the kitchen to grab a *pandesal* from the plastic bag on the counter before rushing out the door with barely a word to anyone. Basti followed him out.

Mom blinked, startled. "Naku, saan nanaman pupunta

'yang kapatid mo na 'yan?" she asked, looking exasperated. "Isa pa 'yang si Martin. Ni hindi makapagtapos ng college. Kung anu-ano kasi ang inaatupag. Pagsabihan mo nga 'yan."

I made an effort to quickly finish washing up so I could escape before my mom could continue, as she often was inclined to do. I grabbed my guitar and raced out of the house while Mom was still in mid-sentence.

Our house was conveniently located right across the barangay plaza where there was a playground, a basketball court, and a small chapel.

I headed for the chapel, my favorite spot for practicing music because of the good enough acoustics.

It was early morning on a Thursday so the area was isolated. Sat down on the chapel's front steps, I strummed my guitar to re-tune it, absently gazing up at our house across the street.

It was definitely not the most opulent on our street, nor the barangay, but I loved it.

It was built in the 1990s when the whole housing area was being developed. The plot of land itself was a loan from one of Mom's aunts.

Mom and Dad had had the foundation of the house built to accommodate a future upgrade into two floors but as fate would have it, due to financial issues, it was never done. Although, we had managed to build small extensions since— an extra room when Martin became a teenager and a wet kitchen.

Still, the house was warm and cozy and I had a lot of happy memories growing up in it.

A big moving truck stole my gaze as it rumbled down the

road and I watched it turn down the street behind the chapel to head to the huge walled-in compound that had *Post No Bills* stamped all across the outside.

The compound had been unoccupied for years, possibly half of my life. But when the truck drove down, the forbidding, rust-colored metal gate that had always been closed, suddenly opened, revealing a peek at the fronting driveway.

The house within was at *least* two floors with Greek-style columns on the front porch. I saw uniformed maids bustling around and gardeners busy tending to the huge garden space inside—just as the large gate closed again.

Kung sino man ang lilipat diyan, malamang talagang big time, I thought with a shrug before I went back to minding my own business.

2

Fiesta Time

"Woo! Maraming salamat!" our lead vocals Boboy Castro called into the microphone after the last song.

Our band's set at the weekend's barangay fiesta was short but given that our band name was "Anywhere/Anytime" suffice it to say, we were of the opinion that any opportunity to perform in public was good.

I had met the rest of the band in college. At the time, we had all easily come together from common situations. That was, we all wished we were taking up a music degree but for various reasons were not.

Boboy was actually a Math major. Shawi on the drums was a P.E. major—yes, those exist. And our lead guitarist, Frank Lloyd, was a Business Econ major.

Our set was after the traditional BINGO and right before the disco which usually lasted for the rest of the night.

To be fair, Barangay San Antonio's feast day fiesta wasn't

exactly the biggest draw for an audience in our genre of music but for us, it really wasn't about the money. (And given that we were being paid peanuts, it really seriously wasn't.)

"Armi, ikaw na muna mag-uwi nung amps, okay?" Boboy called out to me as we finished packing up the rest of our gear into his ancient L300.

I nodded in agreement since I was the obvious choice being that I lived literally meters away.

"Out muna kami, pare." Shawi gave me a high-five before hopping into the front seat of the van.

"Ah, aalis na kayo?" I asked them.

"May gig ang Ben&Ben sa *Rue*," Frank Lloyd shared. "Makiki-inom kami. Enjoy ka muna sa disco night n'yo," he teased with a grin.

"Haha." I made a face. "Thanks, guys," I bid, rapping on the side of the van and watching them drive off before I turned to walk back across the basketball court, passing the BINGO tables being packed away as I headed to the park benches.

Our barangay was family-oriented and always lively during fiesta time. That evening, the basketball court was decorated accordingly with *banderitas*, the requisite glittery disco ball, a couple of modest laser light projectors for the disco, and a refreshments table.

There were also the typical food coupons to be purchased, spot raffle prizes, street food being sold beside the playground, and soft drinks in plastic bags with straws. I actually thought it wasn't too bad.

My best friend Estrella Lucas, Stella for short, was sitting on one bench, eating *chicharon*. "Nice set, Armi," she called out as I arrived.

"Nasaan si Nick?" I asked, looking around for Stella's fiancé before picking up the *chicharon* bag beside her.

"Busy work," Stella replied.

The court lights dimmed and the generic radio music coming over the speakers was quickly replaced by disco music as the "DJ" finished setting up and started with a classic "Mambo No. 5." Some groups of people approached the basketball-court-turned-dance-floor, already cheering.

I spotted Ate Roweena walking up to us from the street. She was still in her uniform, having just come home from the office.

"Hi Ate," I greeted loudly. "Musta work?" I held out the open bag of *chicharon* to her and she took some before responding.

"Toxic."

"May work ka today?" Stella asked Ate Roweena.

"OT," I replied for my sister.

"Idol ka talaga, Weena," Stella piped up, giving her a grin. "Ikaw na yata ang nagpapatakbo ng opisina n'yo eh. Ilang taon ka na doon? Parang kanang kamay ka na ata nung Chairman n'yo."

"Hay nako." Ate Roweena let out a slight groan. "Ako lang kasi ang marunong mag-ayos ng computer sa opisina. Yung iba kong officemate, maski yung mga iPhone nila, hindi nila magamit ng maayos."

"Yesss, si Ate Weena. Maganda na, matalino pa." Stella nodded. "Bakit nga ulit wala ka pa ring boyfriend?"

"Boyfriend? Si Ate? Ew!" I made a face in revulsion.

Stella nudged me pointedly. "Isa ka pa," she chided.

"Nauunahan kasi ng pamumuna. Ibaba mo naman ang kilay mo paminsan, Armi."

I rolled my eyes. "Hmp, sakit sa ulo lang ang mga lalaki, diba 'no, Ate?"

Ate Roweena chuckled. "Naku, mag-ingat ka, Armi," she told me. "Maya-maya 'pag nahanap mo ang katapat mo, malalagot ka talaga."

I stuck my tongue out at my sister and Stella laughed.

Ate Roweena elbowed her. "Ikaw naman, palibhasa lang ikakasal ka na, akala mo naman hindi tatlong taon ang tanda mo sa'kin," she teased.

"Haha." I pointed at Stella in mocking.

Just then, quite a few people turn their heads to look towards the entrance of the basketball court.

I blinked as I noticed. "Anong meron?" I wondered out loud in curiosity, looking over myself.

Stella craned her neck to look and upon easily spotting them in the crowd, she jerked her chin in the direction of the three new arrivals. "Ay, nandiyan na sila," she spoke up with a nod. "'Yung anak ng bagong lipat dun sa compound sa tapat n'yo."

"Ortega nga ba 'yung sabi ni Mommy?" Ate Roweena asked, glancing up to see.

And I realized why the newcomers were getting so much attention. They were so easily distinguishable from the other hundred people in the crowd as all three of them were wearing clothes like they came straight out of fashion magazines, compared to everyone else's maong pants and t-shirts.

I furrowed my eyebrows. "Alin diyan ang Ortega?"

"Yung magkapatid, si Lance sa left at si Cattleya sa right.

Anak sila ni Manuel Ortega, you know, yung may-ari ng BTI tower sa Makati?" Stella relayed.

"Yikes," I muttered as I appraised the small group now venturing forward into the party crowd in the dimly lit basketball court. Then frowning again, I asked next, "Sino yung matangkad na guy sa gitna?"

"Ah, that's Will Salcedo. Nako." Stella smacked my arm in emphasis. "Pamilya nila yung Asia Pacific regional operators ng Spark Energy, may-ari ng HMS Group Holdings, at may-ari ng *Hacienda Salcedo*. Mas mayaman pa sa Diyos. I think best friends sila ni Lance."

"Yikes." I made another face as the three of them passed us by. "Mayaman pa sa Diyos," I echoed in question. "Ano pa naman kaya ang reklamo niya sa buhay at mukhang ang sungit pa rin ng itsura?"

Stella laughed but Ate Roweena shook her head in reprimand. "Armi talaga, ni hindi mo kilala 'yung tao, grabe ka maka-judge."

But I just met Stella's gaze and we both laughed again before she stopped short. "Ay, kausap nila si Papa," she said, her gaze off towards the front of the court. "Tara," she urged, pulling on my hand.

My eyes widened. "Oy," I protested before automatically grabbing Ate Roweena's hand in turn and Stella pulled us towards the refreshments table where Mang Lucas, the Barangay Captain, was talking to the three new arrivals.

Mang Lucas nodded in recognition as Stella arrived with me and Ate Roweena and everyone was briefly introduced. He gestured to me and Ate Roweena as he spoke to Lance, "Sila yung nakatira sa tapat n'yo."

"It's very nice to meet you." Lance gave us a friendly smile.

"Hello po," Ate Roweena greeted with a short nod while I managed a smile back.

"Sayang wala pa yung Mommy at Daddy n'yo," Mang Lucas began to Lance and Cattleya. "Baka next time may pista dito sa'tin, makakasama naman sila."

Lance shrugged, good-naturedly. "Opo, maybe next time."

"O Stella, anak." Mang Lucas turned to her. "I-entertain mo naman muna sila. Baka gusto nila kumain. Meron pa yatang *pichi pichi*, may Coke, may orange juice," he listed before waving and turning to leave to attend to some other business.

Stella watched her father step away, looking a bit uncertain before she turned to Lance, Cattleya, and Will. "Um...you guys hungry?"

I bit my lip to stifle my laughter. I couldn't imagine the three of them being excited about being offered leftover *pichi pichi*.

The expression of displeasure in Cattleya's eyes was plain. Will's gaze was off to one side as if he was pretending he was some other place altogether.

Lance simply gave Stella a smile. "No thanks, Stella. We just had dinner sa labas."

"Alrighty." Stella looked over at Ate Roweena and me and raised her eyebrows as if urging us to initiate some sort of other conversation.

I snapped to attention. "Uh..." I started, looking up at Lance. "Nakita ko pala yung driveway n'yo the other day. Parang ang ganda ng bahay n'yo," I remarked, trying to be nice.

"Yeah, pero our parents are renovating inside. Matagal-tagal na rin kasi hindi na-occupy yung house," Lance relayed.

"The pool is totally gross." Cattleya's nose was wrinkled as she piped up from beside him.

"Oh, may swimming pool kayo?" My eyes lit up.

"Uh, yeah." Lance nodded.

"It's pretty small," Will noted.

"Uh, well of course, compared to the one at your house," Lance pointed out. "Will's house is twice as big as ours," he told everyone.

"At least," Will added flatly.

I shot Will a strange look at his tone but he was still looking off disinterestedly to one side. Cattleya was studying her manicure in the faint light.

"Did I tell you na-meet ko sila nung namanhikan kami kina Nick sa Forbes?" Stella interjected, speaking to Ate Roweena and me then gesturing to them. "That's where they used to live."

Lance narrowed his eyes as he looked at us. "So the two of you live sa kabilang side ng chapel?"

"Oo." I nodded. "May dalawa pa kaming kapatid. Si Martin at si Bingka. Pero nasa dorm na si Martin this weekend. Si Bingka naman, mukhang umuwi na sa bahay." I glanced around to confirm.

Lance turned to Ate Roweena. "So have you always lived here?"

"Yeah," Ate Roweena replied with a friendly smile. "It might be a smaller barangay compared to others pero every-one's very friendly naman."

Lance nodded. "I actually really like it. It feels very close-knit and laid back."

"And it's actually a good area kasi malapit lang sa main road at mga malls," Ate Roweena added.

"Oo nga, I think we passed by an Ayala Mall papunta dito," Lance confirmed with a smile. "You guys probably always hang out there—oh." He stopped short. "Not that I think you only hang out in the mall," he hurried to amend. "I just meant the mall is only like five minutes away."

"Five?" Will repeated dryly. "More like thirty sa traffic, although, I wouldn't discount it."

I shot Will another strange look and Lance noticed.

He chuckled, patting Will's back. "You'll have to excuse my friend. He's a little stressed out from work. He's about to take the reins as COO sa company nila. And right now, he's acting CEO of HMS Group Holdings while his dad is on a business trip to Australia for six months."

"Wow, Australia," I repeated with a vaguely interested nod. "Nakapunta ka na ba doon?" I asked him.

Will replied shortly as though it was obvious, "Of course."

Lance went on, sounding cheerful. "Will's family's company is expanding there and creating what, like four new locations?" he prompted Will.

"At least," Will said again, matter-of-factly.

I resisted the urge to roll my eyes and I just met Stella's gaze again that she had to stifle her laughter.

It was a good thing that Lance, in stark contrast to his friend, was an amiable and friendly guy who seemed happy to carry most of the conversation. It was almost difficult to believe that he and Will were friends at all, let alone best friends.

3

Pinakamaganda

Needing to line up to claim Bingka's raffle prize voucher gave us a much-needed reprieve from the awkward social situation.

"Wow," Stella breathed. "Sa pagka-alala ko hindi naman sila ganoon ka-unfriendly nung na-meet ko sila before. Siguro naninibago lang sa lugar."

"Sigurado ka ba?" I asked in disbelief. "Baka hindi mo lang napansin."

"Anyway," she dismissed with a wave. "Sabi mo ba laging nananalo si Bingka sa raffle?"

"Oo kaya. Remember? In the last few years, nanalo na siya ng isang microwave, isang vacuum cleaner, at pangalawang electric fan na 'to. Matutuwa nanaman si Mommy."

"Wow." Stella whistled. "Swerte nga siya." Then she gave me a wry look. "Masyado ka kasing pessimistic Armi eh. Dapat kasi good vibes ka lagi para nananalo ka rin."

"Kung kailan sakaling gusto ko yung premyo, saka na'ko mag-thi-think positive," I replied and Stella laughed again. "Uy, uy." I tugged on Stella's arm to motion her to look where I was pointing at the dance floor.

Lance was dancing with Ate Roweena.

"Naks, ang powers talaga ni Weena." Stella sounded impressed. "Ikasal na 'yan, dali."

I laughed. "We just met the guy, Stella."

"So what? He's a great catch." Stella shrugged. "Dapat go lang si Weena. Baka maunahan pa siya ng mga iba diyan. Mahirap na."

"Mapili 'yan si Ate," I pointed out. "Who knows? Baka naman she's being nice to him lang kasi new neighbors."

"Well, in fair, bagay sila," Stella observed. "Sayang din ang ganda at talino ni Weena sa kung sinu-sino lang diyan."

"True," I agreed with a nod, giving Stella a high-five.

We must have taken quite a while at the prizes table. On our way back while I was re-reading the prize voucher to make sure I got the right one, Stella pointed out that Lance was ahead of us, having already finished his dance with Ate Roweena. He was talking to Will but because of the thick party crowd, they didn't notice us as we passed by.

"Can we please go now?" Will was urging.

"Wait lang, pare," Lance told him. "I just want to talk to Weena again. She's really nice. Come on, why don't you go talk to the other pretty girls at the party?"

Will sort of coughed. "Seriously? What others?"

Lance elbowed him. "Yung sister in Weena. She's kinda cute rin—si Armi?"

Stella elbowed me with a grin.

But then Will stared at Lance for a few seconds before responding. "Sure."

I shook my head to myself, stifling my laughter. *Grabe, this guy is just so arrogant.*

"It's fun naman, right?" Lance prompted with a smile. "Come on, it's definitely not like the parties we usually go to."

"Understatement," Will replied. "I still don't understand why you wanted to come to this. I mean they couldn't even get proper entertainment. I've never even heard of that band that played kanina. I know it's meant to be indie but seriously?"

And my jaw totally dropped in offense. *What the capital F—?*

Stella laughed under her breath, pulling my arm as we walked faster past them. "Tara na nga, dude."

I huffed in annoyance. "You would think sa dami ng pera n'ya, he can afford some manners."

"Hey look, pasalamat ka na lang hindi siya yung lumipat sa tapat n'yo," Stella pointed out.

The disco "DJ" finished his set with "Despacito" and when microphone feedback came over the speakers, I knew the night was about to deteriorate into drunken videoke by some of the barangay's old timers.

And worse, when I looked up towards where Ate Roweena and Cattleya were, hanging out by the park benches, I saw that my mother was now also there.

"Hala," I mumbled under my breath.

Stella chuckled when she saw what I was looking at. "O siya, mukhang kailangan ka doon," she told me. "Mag-C-CR lang muna ako."

"Whaat?" I made a face in protest.

"Go na," she shooed. "Kawawa naman sila sa nanay mo."

"Kawawa naman *ako*," I muttered hoarsely.

But she just waved me away and I sighed in resignation as I approached them at the same time that Will and Lance came over too.

My mom beamed at them all after she was introduced. "Ay, Lance, anak, sabihin n'yo lang kung kailangan n'yo ng taxi," she said eagerly. "Ipag-da-drive kayo ng asawa ko, maski libre, walang problema."

Lance gave her a small smile. "Thank you po."

"Ganyan talaga dito sa maliit na barangay," my mom went on. "Lahat nagtutulungan. Maliit lang pero masaya naman. Lalo na pag may mga pista. Kine-kwento ko kay Ms. Cattleya kanina, last May *Flores de Mayo* naman."

I shot Ate Roweena a look at the same time that she met my gaze since we both knew what was coming next.

"Alam n'yo ba, si Rowena palagi ang Reyna Elena sa Flores de Mayo," my mom relayed, brimming with pride. "Siyempre, kasi siya ang pinakamaganda sa buong barangay. Siguro maski sa buong Maynila. Lagi kong sinasabi 'yan. Si Rowena ang pinakamaganda sa mga anak ko. At pinakamabait. Mana talaga sa'kin 'yan."

I smirked to myself, watching the vaguely interested expression of Lance and the absolutely disinterested expressions of Cattleya and Will, hoping that at least they actually weren't paying attention to any of this.

But my mom kept going. "Madami-dami na rin manliligaw 'yan. Alam n'yo ba, kahit nga yung pakakasalan nung anak ng Barangay Captain, nanligaw muna kay Rowena 'yon—"

Lance's eyes widened in surprise but it looked like he was just trying to stifle his own laughter.

"Mommy!" Ate Roweena hissed in protest, her own eyes widening in embarrassment.

"Ano?" my mom prompted innocently. "Totoo naman!"

"Ah...eh," I stammered to interrupt very loudly. "Well actually, if you think about it, kung hindi nangyari 'yun, eh di hindi nahanap ni Nick ang soulmate n'ya. And super masaya naman sila ni Stella. So things turned out for the better. Diba ganoon naman talaga minsan?"

"Soulmate?" Will caught the word, giving me a look of ridicule. "You don't really believe in that stuff, do you?"

I pursed my lips, mostly in amusement.

It was like this Will guy was simply intent on having objections to absolutely everything.

"Well." I shrugged modestly. "Simple lang naman kami dito. We're willing to concede na may mga bagay sa mundo na hindi namin talaga control," I reasoned, pausing for a second. "But I guess some people can afford to take that for granted, diba 'no?"

And I beamed my sunniest smile at everyone.

* * *

I was practicing guitar in our room later that night after the party when Ate Roweena came in to get ready for bed. I stopped to look up at her. "So?"

She shot me a look. "So ano?"

I wiggled my eyebrows suggestively. "So kayo na ni Lance?"

Ate Roweena gave me a look of ridicule. "Nakikipagsocialize lang naman yung tao kanina. Puro talaga malisya ang utak mo."

I rolled my eyes. "Pleeez Ate, ikaw lang naman ang sinayaw n'ya 'no," I reminded her. "And halos ikaw lang ang kinausap buong gabi. Wag mo nang i-deny, may gusto ka rin naman sa kanya."

"Kailan ko naman sinabi 'yon?" she asked defensively. "Ang sabi ko lang kanina mabait siya, may itsura, maayos manamit—"

"At mayaman. Jackpot ka, sister!" I quipped.

Ate Roweena threw a pillow at me. "Ikaw talaga! As if naman pera lang ang nakikita ko sa lalaki 'no? Siyempre dapat muna mabait."

"Ewan ko ba sa'yo. Lahat naman ng tao para sa'yo mabait. Weirdo ka."

"Pwera si Will," Ate Roweena spoke up with a laugh and a look of shock on her face. "I still can't believe sinabi n'ya 'yun tungkol sa'yo."

"I know, right? And ano siya, expert on indie bands?"

"Hayaan mo na lang," she bade. "Hindi lang naman ikaw ang nakapansin na hindi siya friendly at na super mayabang siya. Maski si Mommy parang narinig ko kanina. *Hinayupak na yabang* daw."

"Hmp. Hayaan ko sana yung super yabang niya kung hindi lang siya malakas mang-insulto. Whatevs," I dismissed. "In any case, malamang hindi na naman natin makikita ulit 'yon. Who cares na lang?"

Ate Roweena pursed her lips, shrugging silently but looking as though she was thinking of something else.

And after a pause, I gave her another mischievous look. "Buti pa si Lance mabait 'no?"

Ate Roweena met my gaze blankly. "Ha?"

"'To talaga si Ate," I teased. "Kung hindi mo siya crush, ako na lang, crush ko siya."

And she laughed again.

4

Ulan

"Carmina!" my mom's voice sailed throughout the house, easily over the sound of the falling rain outside, early on a Friday morning.

Still in bed, I groaned as I rolled over. "Bakit po?"

"Diba may pasok ka ngayon?" Mom called out again. "Bilisan mo na't kailangan ko rin pumunta sa City Hall. Kailangan daw nila ng tulong sa opisina."

I opened one eye to check the time from my phone beside my bed before groaning again, begrudgingly pushing up off the bed to get ready.

I was temporarily waitressing at Pancake House just to make enough money while I looked for a "real" job.

I liked it because the job was relatively easy. It gave me time for my music. As well as I had specifically managed to wrangle a three-day-a-week shift.

Also, of course, I loved pancakes.

My family was at the breakfast table while I brushed my teeth.

"Ilang araw na 'yang ulan na 'yan," my dad was saying, sounding displeased. "Siguradong grabe nanaman ang traffic. Lalo na't hindi pa tapos yung construction sa EDSA."

"Kahit sa MRT n'yo na lang ako ihatid, Dad," Ate Roweena replied. "Para naman hindi na kayo mahirapan."

"Oo nga pala, Rowena!" my mom spoke up, sounding thrilled. "Hindi mo naman sinabi, nagsayaw daw pala kayo ni Lance nung disco sa pista nung isang linggo ha? Nakwento lang sa'kin ni Mrs. Roldan kanina."

She went on with a loud excited sigh. "Ay, buti ka pa, mayaman ang mapapang-asawa mo. Trabahuhin mo 'yan anak ha, nang hindi ka matulad sa'kin."

"Ma!" Ate Roweena exclaimed in protest just as I came out to the dining room. I met her gaze and laughed to myself.

My dad was somewhat (wisely) only half-paying attention to the conversation with his head buried behind his coffee and the *Inquirer* as per usual.

I ruffled Bingka's hair in greeting then reached past her to take a piece of *pandesal* from the table to put in the oven toaster before standing by to wait, watching both my dad and Ate Roweena shake their heads from my mom's sentiments in the meantime.

Mom noticed and made a show of shrugging. "Ang ibig ko lang naman sabihin, gusto ko sana matiyak na maaliwalas ang kalagayan n'yong magkakapatid kapag wala na kami ng tatay n'yo," she explained.

"Saan kayo pupunta, Mommy?" Bingka gave her a

prompting look, her spoonful of *tocino* and rice stopped half-way to her mouth.

My dad and I exchanged glances and I grinned before I changed the subject. "'Ngapala Mommy, Daddy, nag-text po pala si Martin sa'kin," I relayed. "Uuwi daw siya mamayang gabi."

"Mag-co-commute lang ba siya ?" Dad asked. "Ipaalala mo sa kanya, bahain yung lugar nila."

"Mommy, na-check n'yo rin po ba 'yung announcements sa school ni Bingka?" Ate Roweena asked as she hurried Bingka along to finish her meal. "Nung isang linggo, binaha din yung school, diba po?"

"Hindi pa ba kasali yung eskwelahan nila sa text alert?" Mom walked over to the TV to quickly check the news.

Just then Ate Roweena sneezed three times in a row, at the same time that the toaster dinged.

I shot her a look to ask, "O, okay ka lang, Ate?" before I went to get my bread.

"Oo," she dismissed. "Nahamugan yata ako. Ilang araw na ako sinisipon."

"Vitamins mo, Rowena," Mom called out, holding out a little container.

"Thanks, Ma," Ate Roweena said, taking some capsules even as she sniffled some more.

My dad's forehead creased. "Sigurado kang papasok ka, Weena? Malakas pa rin ang ulan. Baka mabinat ka lang lalo."

"May importanteng training po today eh," Ate Roweena replied, blowing her nose. "As usual, ako lang nanaman ang may alam kung paano gawin." She shook her head with a sigh.

I had to ask, "Para saan pa ang SL mo kung hindi mo naman ginagamit?"

"Weekend na naman," she assured everyone. "Sa Monday na lang, kung masama pa rin pakiramdam ko."

My mouth full, I just shrugged as I chewed.

"O, handa na ba kayong lahat?" Dad asked as he stood, folding up his newspaper before heading for the door.

My eyes lit up in alert. "Ay teka!" I stuffed the rest of my *pandesal* in my mouth before grabbing my bag and following everyone out.

* * *

I spent Friday night, as per usual, hanging out with my band at one of the local bars where we always tried to get the owners to give us a regular spot.

Afterwards, we all headed over to Boboy's house to jam with his sister Jen who sometimes played keyboards with us.

I didn't come home until way past midnight, so naturally, I woke up late the next morning.

By the time I came out to the dining room, Martin was the only one at the table, his iPhone in his hand, his other hand shoving Coco Puffs from a bowl into his mouth. Basti was asleep at his feet.

I could hear Mom out by the gate talking to one of the neighbors and I knew Dad and Bingka had gone to the mall to pay some bills.

I stood beside the dining table, trying to decide if I could be bothered to make some breakfast for myself since everyone else had already finished. I asked Martin carelessly, "Nasaan si Ate?"

"Nasa kapitbahay ata sabi ni Mommy," Martin mumbled between mouthfuls.

I furrowed my eyebrows in puzzlement. "Ha? Ang aga naman." I paused to try to recall if I had seen her in our room all night at all. "Parang hindi ko siya narinig magising kanina a."

"Dumaan yung Cattleya kagabi, nagpatulong mag-ayos ng computer," he relayed briefly, shoving his long hair back from his face.

My eyes widened. "Ano? Ibig mong sabihin hindi umuwi si Ate kagabi?" I prompted just as Mom walked back into the house.

"Ay Carmina, tumawag kagabi si Sir Lance," my mom told me. "I think may sakit nga daw Ate mo. Naisip ko mabuti pa nandoon na lang siya. Siguradong mas mahal at mas magagaling ang mga doktor nila."

I rolled my eyes in exasperation. "Mommy," I rasped. "Ni hindi n'yo man lang pinuntahan?"

"Nag-text naman sa'kin si Rowena kagabi," Mom rationalized. "Okay lang naman daw siya, at nasa kapitbahay lang naman siya, ang lapit-lapit."

I blew out a breath, already getting ready to leave, grabbing my wallet and my keys.

Unfortunately, I knew my mother well enough to know that she was trying to make sure we—and by we, I meant, my Ate Roweena—insinuated ourselves into the lives of our next-door neighbors as much as possible. And while I did admire my mother's focus and goal-orientedness, sometimes they overrode her sense of propriety.

"Payong, 'tol," Martin called out.

"Ambon lang naman." I waved as I headed out the door.

5

❧

Katapat

The person who answered the doorbell at *214 San Antonio Avenue* let me into the little door in the big gate, and I walked cautiously up the sloped driveway towards the dauntingly large front porch where I'd been directed.

The house looked even bigger up close. The driveway was lined with well-manicured rows of plants and color-coded *bougainvillea* flowers. The Bermuda grass looked absolutely flawless.

I gawked at the two fancy cars parked along the driveway as I walked past them. I narrowed my eyes as I read some letters off the backs. '*SLK*' on the Mercedez and '*BRZ*' on the Subaru. I whistled. I had no idea what the letters meant but the cars sure were shiny.

Hanging plants and the giant chandelier from inside were visible through the huge round windows on the front of the house. There also seemed to be some construction work going on in the back of the house. A hint of a scaffold could be seen even from the driveway and there was a pile of building materials covered under a plastic sheet by the side of the garden.

I finally got to the front porch, the floor of which was an elaborate tile mosaic of the sun. I belatedly noticed that the doorknob was made of crystal-like glass and gold-plating when I pushed the front door open.

The inside of the house looked like a hotel/resort lobby. There were Filipino-themed paintings on the walls, classy wooden art sculptures, shiny glass mirrors, staircases both to the left and right of the front door which must lead to the rooms upstairs.

And right in front of me, past the foyer, was another wide but short staircase headed down towards a split-level open-plan living area where there was a *second* giant chandelier.

I nearly whistled when I saw the grand piano in the corner then gawked upon seeing that past it was another set of sliding glass doors, leading to the big beautiful swimming pool in the back of the house.

I had stopped at the top of the wide staircase, stunned for a moment before I snapped to attention upon spotting Will and Cattleya sitting in the living area downstairs.

Will was at a desk, frowning over a laptop. Cattleya was on her phone, sitting on the couch.

I looked around for Lance but couldn't see him anywhere. I tentatively cleared my throat, loud enough for Will and Cattleya to notice.

And when they did, they both stared up at me, looking surprised.

"Nice hair," Cattleya decided to comment with a smirk.

Self-conscious, I ran my fingers through my frizzy damp bob to fix it before giving them both a sheepish look. "Uh...hi." I waved. "Nandito daw po si—"

"Sa taas." Will pointed to the staircase to the left before I even finished my question.

I blinked. "Um, thanks." I shrugged, turning to head to the staircase, almost running into Lance on his way down.

"Hey, Armi! I was just about to go to your house," Lance spoke up, looking surprised himself.

"Hi..." I noted the worried look on his face. "Anong nang-yari kay Ate?"

He beckoned me upstairs as he explained that Ate Roweena had fainted while she was trying to fix Cattleya's computer last night. She had run a high fever and they had put her into one of the guest rooms.

"Don't worry," Lance assured me. "One of our maids is a nurse. She's been looking in on Weena all night."

I nodded as I followed him towards the guest room. "Sala-mat ha," I told him with a small smile. "Pasensya na sa abala."

"It's no problem at all," he assured with a smile. "At least she was here and not out commuting or somewhere else, right?" he said as he gestured me to the room. "I'm sure Weena just needs to rest for a while. Why don't you go see her muna and then you can come down and wait sa living room. Will and Catt are also there," he bid cheerfully before turning to go first.

I hid my grimace but nodded in reply before I entered the room. My sister was tucked into what was an actual four-poster bed with a nurse sitting by her side.

Ate Roweena's eyes lit up upon seeing me. "Armi!" she cried out, looking relieved. "Uwi na tayo!"

I laughed before looking over at the nurse.

She introduced herself as Ate Jasmine and informed me that Ate Roweena's fever had already broken and that she just needed to be monitored for another couple of hours before being allowed to come home with me.

I thanked Ate Jasmine and apologized again. It was unlikely that her actual job responsibilities included caring for random sick neighbors.

Once Ate Jasmine had left the room, I met Ate Roweena's gaze again.

"Oh my god, kagabi pa'ko nahihiya dito," she confessed, sounding distressed. "I can't believe nahimatay ako habang tumitingin ng computer ni Cattleya."

I shook my head. "Sinabi kasi kahapon na huwag ka nang pumasok eh," I reprimanded lightly. "Anyway, mukhang natutuwa naman si Lance na nandito ka. Although—" I paused for effect, giving her a knowing look. "Siyempre, mas natutuwa si Mommy."

And we both laughed.

6

Ang Peg

Lance had started playing an Xbox game by the time I got back downstairs. Will and Cattleya had barely moved.

"Dude, what's the point of hanging out with us if you're just going to work anyway?" Lance's question to Will sounded exasperated despite him not looking up from the game he was occupied with.

Will cast him a glance before focusing back on his laptop as he presumably dealt with business. "Just don't," he replied shortly.

Lance noticed me arrive and he looked up with a smile before pausing his game. "Hey Armi, kamusta si Weena?"

I gave him a short reassuring nod. "She's fine daw sabi ni Ate Jasmine. She's just sleeping it off now. Don't worry, uuwi na kami pag-gising n'ya," I assured.

Lance shrugged, still smiling. "Hey, no problem, there's no rush." He gestured to his game. "Do you want to play *Halo*?"

he offered. "Or there's a billiards table in the game room. TV?" He pointed to several things.

I gave him a quick appreciative smile. "Thanks, okay lang ako. I'll just wait here." I nodded, gesturing to my phone. My *chipipay* internet plan was about to prove itself.

"Upo ka muna." Lance waved before hitting un-pause on his game.

I sat down on the other end of the couch from where Cattleya was sitting. She looked at me, not saying anything, and I felt compelled to start a conversation. "Kamusta na 'yung computer mo?" I asked, trying to sound polite.

Cattleya gave me what looked like a forced smile back. "It's fine. Weena's really good," she replied, though sounding by no means interested in continuing the conversation. She stood up to stand by Will to look over his shoulder.

"Wow, Will, you have so many emails," Cattleya noted. "Is that all for work? I can't imagine having to deal with so many boring emails." She wrinkled her nose.

Will just cleared his throat, not looking pleased with the audience but not saying anything either.

I had started reading on my phone, not paying them any attention, but Cattleya was making a show of sighing, looking bored and it was mildly amusing to observe Will's reactions to Cattleya's attention-seeking behavior.

"Hey, can you video chat Monica?" Cattleya piped up. "Tell her I got that video she sent from when she was at that Dance Academy Recital."

"Pwede later, Catt," Will spoke up. "I have to finish this. Besides, didn't you chat with her last night?"

"Okay." Cattleya rolled her eyes in resignation. She glanced over at Lance blankly, quickly determining that she would get no attention there either before finally she turned to me again.

"Hey Armi, do you know Will's sister, Monica? She's like a sister to me too," she relayed animatedly. "She's awesome. Like she's super talented. She dances ballet. She can sing. She models," she boasted as if the achievements were actually her own.

I had to nod. "Wow."

"She also plays the piano and takes violin lessons," Cattleya went on. "She speaks *four* languages. She's almost a black belt in Karate and plays soccer too. She's a really amazing girl."

"Wow," I said again with a small, curious frown. "Ang dami."

"Oh, Will's parents are having her do *everything*," Cattleya said dismissively.

My eyes widened. "Wow," I said yet again before I asked something apparently unexpected. "Why?"

Cattleya and Will both shot me a look. Lance only glanced up from his game, only half-paying attention to the conversation.

When Will replied, his tone was more like puzzled disbelief. "My parents believe in giving her the best possible start," he declared. "These are important skills to have for achieving success in life."

I kept nodding, mostly in resignation as I didn't want to start a debate. "Sure, wow, okay." I shrugged. "These are important skills for achieving success in life," I repeated mechanically.

Cattleya was giving me a veiled annoyed look as I had

managed to extract more words from Will so far than she had possibly all morning. "Will's parents' dream is for him to marry a girl just as successful," she interjected with a smug, knowing smile. "Hindi pupuwede ang maski sino lang diyan."

Will cleared his throat again, looking uncomfortable with the topic of conversation.

"Wow." I whistled, shaking my head to comment, "Ang tarik naman ng definition ng 'successful'."

"Will's family has very high standards," Cattleya added cattily.

I wasn't actually sure whether she was trying to indicate that *she* herself fits the bill or that she was saying that I was obviously definitely *not* under consideration.

Regardless, I leaned towards Lance slightly to whisper not-so-quietly. "Let me guess, he's still single?" I asked in mocking and Will shot me a dark look.

But Lance just laughed.

I put my hands up in defeat again. "Sorry." I laughed myself. "Para lang kasing hindi realistic yung peg."

Will frowned at me but before he could say anything, Cattleya came over to sit with me.

"Hey Armi," she began, suddenly with a bright disposition as though we were old friends as she held up her phone.

"Let's take a picture. May bago akong social media filters. They're super cute," she gushed, angling her face beside mine to take several photos, barely even giving me a chance to respond, her phone camera already clicking away.

"See?" She showed me some photos before then holding the phone out towards Lance and Will to show them.

Lance gave the phone a cursory glance but Will didn't

move. Cattleya watched him with a prompting smile. "Will, you want to join us?" she coaxed sweetly.

Will shrugged, focusing again on still not looking away from his laptop screen. "I suppose you never read that article about the personality disorders of people who take too many selfies."

Cattleya blinked bemusedly, looking up at Lance then me in turn. "Aww, what do you guys suppose he's trying to imply?"

I shook my head, knowing full well Will was gearing up to *insulto*-mode again. "Wag mo nga tanungin," I told Cattleya. "Feeling ko magsisisi lang tayo. Parang tayo pa naghanap ng pang-asar sa mga sarili natin."

Lance burst out laughing again. "You're so funny, Armi."

"Well, you know." I grinned, pleased that at least someone else was amused. "It helps not to take myself too seriously," I added meaningfully, tilting my head in Will's direction but not saying anything outright.

"Ay, no." Lance shook his head. "Bawal tuksuhin 'yan si Will," he said mischievously.

I pursed my lips, meeting Will's gaze. "Oo nga naman pala," I declared. "'Cause, of course, you're perfect, right?"

"And proud of it!" Lance interjected with a grin even as he was still playing his game.

"I never said I was perfect," Will declared. "I just believe it's better to aspire for perfection than it is to settle for mediocrity. I actually also happen to think that pride is warranted when you're around mediocrity."

"And by 'mediocrity', you're referring to people less superior to you," I guessed.

"Which is everyone," Will stated directly.

"*Of course*," I remarked with a nod, almost wondering why I was even still surprised.

7

Benitez's

Cattleya had become bored with the conversation, being that it wasn't centered on her. She had walked upstairs towards the foyer windows to look out to the garden, watching the rain that was intermittently falling. Then after a few minutes, she wrinkled her nose. "Who is that?" she asked, holding back the curtains.

I glanced over at Will and Lance who seemed less interested before I walked upstairs myself to have a look.

I stopped short when I thought I saw Bingka's head of French-braided hair peering into the small door in the big front gate which had been left open. "Bingka!" I spoke up.

"Who?" Cattleya asked.

"Um, bunsong kapatid namin," I told her then my eyes widened as Bingka strolled right into the gate before another head poked into the door in the gate. "Martin!" I said again.

"Who?" Cattleya asked again, and by this time, Lance had walked up to us by the window to look as well.

"Um, uh, brother ko," I explained sheepishly. I watched as Martin tried to wave Bingka to come back before he himself stepped cautiously into the gate.

Then yet *another* head poked into the door in the gate. "Oh shit, si Mommy," I muttered, making a face.

Cattleya stifled her laughter, casting me a funny look. "Is your whole entire family coming?"

I actually wouldn't have been surprised if my dad came in after them with Basti at his heels but I didn't reply. Instead, I rushed to the door to meet them.

Bingka was already at the porch when I opened the door a crack. "Hi Ate!" she greeted cheerfully, holding up some flowers. "Look, bugambilya!"

"Bingka," I reprimanded lightly. "Bakit mo naman pinitas 'yan? Hindi natin garden 'to." I looked up as my mom reached the porch with Martin. "Mommy, anong ginagawa n'yong lahat dito?"

My mom gave me an innocent look. "Susunduin lang naman sana namin kayo," she answered, trying to peer into the slight gap in the door behind me. "Mag-ta-tanghalian na..." she said, obviously curious to see inside the house.

That's when Lance came up behind me and opened the door full. "Good afternoon po," he greeted them all with a smile.

"Ay, Lance, anak." My mom gave him a big smile. "Kaka-mustahin lang sana namin si Weena. Sana naman hindi masyadong malaking abala sa inyo at naaalagaan siya ng mabuti."

"Of course naman po," Lance replied. "Wala pong abala. Pasok po kayo." He beckoned them all to come in.

Mom looked delighted as she eagerly stepped through the door past him, looking up and around. "Wow chandelier!" she couldn't help but exclaim upon spotting the chandelier in the foyer then she stopped short again as she saw the other one across the room. "Wow, *dalawang* chandelier!"

Will had gone to stand silently by the sliding doors. Cattleya was back sitting on the couch in the living room, watching us as we all came downstairs.

"Upo muna po kayo." Lance gestured to the couch. "Sabi yata ni Armi, malapit na'ng pwedeng umuwi si Weena." He cast me a glance to confirm.

I nodded. "Yeah. Pag-gising daw niya, uwi na *tayong lahat*," I said, looking at my mom pointedly as she and Bingka sat on the couch opposite Cattleya.

"Your house is very nice," Mom gave Cattleya a smile. "Nakita ko yata sa magasin sa grocery itong coffee table ninyo. Mukhang luma. Antique?"

Cattleya just gave her a curt nod and a small smile in acknowledgment.

I noticed that Cattleya seemed distracted watching Martin warily as he was wandering around the huge, expensively-furnished room, peering closely at things on shelves.

I resisted the urge to roll my eyes. I didn't even want to venture a guess about what Cattleya was thinking right then.

When Cattleya didn't seem keen to continue the conversation, my mom turned to Lance again. "Maraming salamat nga pala ulit, Lance," my mom said. "Paano ba kami magpapasala-mat sa pag-alaga n'yo sa anak ko?" she asked then her eyes lit up. "Minsan, mag-hapunan kayo sa amin! Ipaghahanda ko kayo ng paborito n'yong pagkain," she suggested.

Lance chuckled good-naturedly. "Don't worry po, Tita. Walang anuman po 'yon. Di po ba sabi n'yo, ganyan talaga dito sa maliit na barangay. Lahat nagtutulungan?"

My mom beamed at him, looking pleased again then she looked around. "Nasaan pala ang mga magulang n'yo? Gusto ko rin silang pasalamatan."

Cattleya volunteered a reply. "They're staying at our condo this week. Kasi it's so expensive to drive back and forth from here to civilization," she said, almost stifling a chuckle.

I blinked, looking quickly at my mom.

Fortunately, she was much too impressed with the house to be offended by any snide comments. Instead, she just replied with a matter-of-fact tone, "Malapit lang naman. Lalo na't nandyan lang ang pasukan sa Skyway."

Lance was giving Cattleya a meaningful look. "Oo nga naman," he said firmly. "Hindi naman ganoon kalayo. Diba 'no, Will?"

Will blinked as though slightly surprised to have been asked to support this claim. "Technically, the Skyway is like seventeen kilometers to Makati CBD where everyone is." He looked over at me briefly as if to punctuate his statement before looking away again.

I shook my head. *Such a show-off...*

But my mom was not fazed. "Wala namang magkaka-kilala sa Makati. Buti pa dito sa amin, magkakakilala ang mga magka-kapitbahay. At walang suplado," she added so noncha-lantly that I almost laughed out loud but my mom went on without missing a beat. "Bale, pakisabi na lang sa mga magulang n'yo, anak, maraming salamat," she told Lance with another smile.

"Of course po." Lance nodded, himself trying to let the comment about Will slide without chuckling. "Pero they'll definitely be here at the end of the month," he relayed. "For my birthday."

Bingka, who had been contentedly making a flower chain with her *bougainvillea* flowers on the couch brightened when she heard Lance's last statement. "Talaga po? August baby ka? August baby rin po ako! Mag-bi-birthday party kayo dito sa house n'yo? Invite n'yo po kami ha?"

Lance blinked, having been caught off-guard. "Um..."

I shot Lance a quick apologetic look first before I looked over at Bingka in light reprimand. "Bingka, 'wag mo naman biglain si Kuya Lance."

"Birthday n'ya eh," Bingka replied as though logically. "Siyempre mag-bi-birthday party siya. Sabado po ha? Para wala akong pasok kinabukasan."

I caught Martin's gaze of disbelief across the room as it mirrored my own. But Bingka was a force to be reckoned with. Often nobody could stop her when she was being ridiculously adorable.

Either way, it seemed to work on Lance. He smiled at her brightly. "Sige ba," he told her. "Gusto mo 'pag magaling na ang Ate Weena mo, sabihin mo sa'kin kailan mo gusto mag-party."

My mom was so happy, she was still in thrills even after Ate Roweena woke up and was ready to go home. She, Bingka, and Martin walked ahead down the driveway to go back to the house.

I walked past Cattleya on my way out as she was thanking Ate Roweena for fixing her computer and I noted amusedly, that it seemed that Cattleya's smile looked genuine that time. I supposed it was a good sign that at least she liked Ate Roweena.

I stopped a few steps away from the porch to watch as Ate Roweena next said goodbye to Lance at the door. I smiled to myself again, satisfied that I could sense there was a comfortable air between them and my smile widened when I saw Lance taking down Ate Roweena's number on his phone.

Then I glanced past the two of them to see Cattleya and Will standing back inside the foyer, both looking as sullen as ever.

I shook my head in mirth, thrusting my hand up in a peace sign before yelling loudly, "Bye!" as I turned and left.

8

Handa

When Mang Lucas hosted a *pakain* one weekend evening to celebrate Stella's upcoming wedding, practically the entire barangay had been invited. There were people enough to fill their pale green two-story house, as well as had spilled onto the street in front.

There was a lot of laughing, noisy chatting, and general merriment in the air. A videoke machine was set up in the garage and someone was belting out a very loud, very heartfelt but slightly out-of-tune, rendition of "Rain" by Donna Cruz.

Bingka was in the garden, playing *piko* with some of the neighborhood kids. Stella's mom, Aling Roz, was at the gate, standing by a smoking grill, making pork barbecue and hotdogs, gossiping with some of the other "Titas" from our street.

I was trying to stay out of the chaos, hanging out at the balcony on the second floor with Martin, leaning over the railing and watching the goings-on downstairs. I spotted my mom and dad walking past below and overheard what they were talking about.

"Hay nako Rene," my mom was groaning out loud. "Alam mo bang nag-drop nanaman kaagad ng subject ang anak mo?" she asked. "Pagsasabihan mo ba siya tungkol sa pag-aaral n'ya?"

"Gusto mo ba pagsabihan ko siya?" my dad responded, using his usual diversionary tactic of putting the question back to my mom.

Mom sighed in exasperation. "Akala niya yata madali lang kumita ng pera ngayon."

I chuckled, looking over my shoulder at Martin. "Pinapag-awayan ka nanaman nila Mommy."

Martin glanced up at me from his seat, slumped on the rattan couch with his iPhone in his hand as usual. "What's new?" he remarked curtly before going back to *Fortnite*.

I shook my head at him in reprimand. "Hay nako Martin. Kung bawat sem, mag-shi-shift ka ng course, paano ka mag-tatapos?" I prompted expectantly. "Tignan mo ako, four years lang. Express college. Hindi ko ginustong magtagal doon."

"Eh paano, ni hindi mo naman ginusto yung course mo, eh," Martin pointed out, not looking up. "At least ako, gusto ko mahanap yung course na gusto ko talaga." He shrugged. "Hindi ko pa nga lang nahahanap."

I made a face at Martin, even though he wasn't looking, before looking back down at my parents.

"—yung trabaho sa construction," my mom was still going on.

"Oo na nga," my dad replied. "Dadaan daw siya mamaya

o bukas para pag-usapan namin kung papaano aayusin yung utang."

"Baka kulangin tayo ng oras, Rene," my mom was saying. "Yung bahay—"

My dad sighed again. "Alam ko, Adel. Hindi nakakatulong ang sobrang pag-alala."

My forehead creased with a curious feeling of apprehension. It almost sounded like we were having bigger money problems than usual, bigger problems than what my parents were letting on.

Worried, I cast a glance over at Martin again. Especially if Martin didn't get his act together.

Not to mention, if *I* didn't manage to get a stable, proper-paying job, I also thought, a wave of guilt coming over me.

I pushed off the balcony railing and headed down via the back staircase, intending to fish for more information from my parents.

But I stopped short, almost running into someone heading up the stairs, blocking my way.

I blinked in surprise when I recognized him. "Will."

He met my gaze. "Hi."

I looked past his shoulder to see that Ate Roweena had arrived with Lance. Cattleya was begrudgingly following behind the two of them.

"O, kakadating n'yo lang ba?" I asked Will.

Will stepped back down the stairs to let me pass. "Yeah."

It had been almost three weeks since Ate Roweena had passed out trying to fix Cattleya's computer and since then, as far as I knew, Ate Roweena and Lance had been regularly meeting up, texting every day, the whole nine yards. It was a rare occasion when she didn't mention his name in conversation.

And I was mostly happy for her.

Except for, unfortunately, this also meant that we saw more of super yabang Will.

I was starting to wonder if maybe Will was actually Lance's body guard or chaperone or something. Lance rarely went anywhere without him.

Will, of course, was still the same frigid, unfriendly bastard. He never initiated conversations, only spoke when spoken to, and often only said things that were insulting or insensitively blunt.

I always tried not to be daunted by him. If he thought he could push us around just because we didn't have as much money as him, he was majorly wrong. Plus, it was incredibly gratifying every time I stumped him when he was being an arrogant show-off.

I gave Will a once-over look.

Tonight, he was wearing a business-casual designer suit again. His shirt was from the monogram-printed new Burberry collection. Granted, he looked *super cute*. It even looked like he had made the slightest amount of effort to fix up his hair tonight.

But his outfit choices always seemed to hint that he had absolutely no other clothes in his closet or he just didn't understand how to dress for these kinds of parties. Or perhaps, it was that he simply wanted everyone to know he really did not belong here.

"Nice shirt," I remarked with a smirk before I stepped past him towards the front door where Ate Roweena was headed.

Ate Roweena and Lance were in the living room with Stella and Nick and a couple of other friends. And as Will and I walked over to them, I could already hear Nick telling stories about *Tita*.

"Tita is just such a magnanimous person," Nick was saying. "She gave us some party tips for the wedding reception and na-kwento ko ba na she's even hosting a dinner for Stella and me, for the wedding?"

I wasn't really interested in Nick's long-winded stories. And being that Will and Cattleya were around, I definitely knew being insulted was not far into my future.

So I was intending to pull Stella *away* from said group, but as soon as I got within arm's reach, she put her arm around my shoulders instead.

Possibly she was mistaking my intention to want to hang out with her little circle. Either that or it was an indication for me to stick around just so she wasn't driven stir-crazy by the company herself.

"Sinong Tita 'yan?" Porscha, one of Stella's other friends wanted to know.

Already groaning under my breath, I met Ate Roweena's identical knowing gaze. *Here we go.*

Nick's eyes lit up.

The rest of us had all but gotten sick of his stories about his family's next-door neighbor since they had moved to

Forbes a few years ago. But Nick was always eager to share stories about *Tita*.

I'd never met her of course and personally, I'd always thought that Nick's stories about how close he and *Tita* were were likely wildly exaggerated. But ever since Nick and Stella got engaged last year, it was as though we could never have enough of Nick singing her praises.

In any case, from what I'd gathered so far, her house was like a huge Spanish villa. And she was no doubt as rich as her name sounded.

"Si Donya Viuda Felicitacion Villareal San Mateo," Nick recited in full, proudly. "But she told me to just call her Tita. She's helped my parents so much since we moved next door sa kanila. She always says hi to me."

"Wow." Porscha's eyes widened, looking impressed already. "Ang swerte mo naman. Parang ang bait nga n'ya."

Nick nodded eagerly. "Yeah. Diba 'no, Will?" He glanced up at Will. "Will is Tita's inaanak sa binyag," he relayed to Porscha.

Will only gave him a small nod of acknowledgment but said nothing.

"Hmm." Porscha gave Will a small uncomfortable smile.

I hid my own smile.

Obviously, by this time, Will—or rather Will's anti-social behavior—was well-known around the barangay and his reputation already preceded him. Though I hadn't known that he was related to Nick's favorite *Tita*. That was an interesting development.

"Her daughter Graciella is also nice," Stella piped up brightly.

"Yeah." Nick nodded again. "Sayang lang, she doesn't go out much. She's a bit sakitin. I told her nga na the boys are missing out kasi if she went out, she would have so many manliligaw for sure." He winked. "I told her I could really tell she was brought up in a very well-to-do environment. She's very classy and elegant." He smiled yet again. "Of course, nagustuhan naman niya yung compliment ko. I really know what girls want to hear, diba babe?" He leaned over to kiss Stella's cheek.

I couldn't help but interject since I totally knew better, "Yeah and ang pag-deliver mo pa, halos parang hindi obvious na puro bola lang."

Ate Roweena, Stella, and her friends all stifled their laughter but Nick simply gave me an unfazed look. "Armi talaga, of course I meant it," he maintained. "You know naman me. I mean I wouldn't say so myself, but I'm a super genuine person. Everyone says so."

I bit my lip in mirth but before anyone could say anything more, Mang Lucas walked up to us. "O Stella, anak, Nick," he greeted over the din. "Wala bang kakanta sa inyo? Kanina pa dun si Axel. Maawa naman kayo sa mga kapitbahay natin."

"Mamaya na lang, Pa," Stella replied with a dismissive wave.

But Mang Lucas gave everyone in the circle a prompting look anyway.

"No thank you po," Lance declined with a polite smile.

"Ikaw Armi, sige na." Mang Lucas urged me with a beckon. "Siguradong gusto ka rin marinig nila Sir Lance, Sir Will."

I chuckled in skepticism. "I don't think 'sigurado' 'yon, Tito."

Will's shrug was nonchalant. "Actually, I wouldn't mind."

I blinked up at him in surprise.

"As long as you can do better than this," he added his reason, referring to the current cat wailing.

"Oo, magaling 'yan si Armi," Mang Lucas cheered, turning to me. "'Diba nga may banda kayo, iha?"

"Oh?" Will met my gaze.

I blinked at him, reserving my ire. "Narinig mo na kami. Kami yung banda na tumugtog sa pista last month. Naalala mo 'yon?" I prompted sweetly, pointedly.

Stella's eyes popped wide open in alarm and Ate Roweena's nails dug into my arm.

But Will barely flinched. He shrugged again, "Hmm," and didn't even so much as offer an apology before he excused himself and walked away from the group.

9

Walang hiya hiya

"Ha? Sinong ikakasal? Si Stella?"

The brusque voice at the door made practically everyone downstairs look over.

I groaned the instant I saw who had arrived and I mumbled only enough for Ate Roweena and Stella on either side of me to hear. "Ah shet, nandito si Tito Boy."

It was a legendary statistical oddity that every Filipino family has a "Tito Boy." Personally, I didn't know how true that was. My dad's cousin's full name was Joselito Vicente Domingo but in any case, everyone called him "Boy."

Tito Boy was a loud man. And if he had an opinion, you would soon know it. It was often shallow, often ignorant, and at times selfish.

My dad had lived with his family upon his first arrival in Manila, so unfortunately, we owed Tito Boy quite a lot.

He was one of those inescapable relations you wished you didn't have.

Throughout the years, Tito Boy had managed to build or acquire several small businesses, including the taxi service, as well as a relatively successful construction company.

He thought of himself as quite the big-time guy. So it wasn't surprising at all, not to me anyway, that he had decided to "crash" Stella's party.

But naturally, Mang Lucas was a very gracious host. And as per usual practice in the Philippines, it was always "the more, the merrier."

Tito Boy walked over to our group with Mom, Dad and Martin with this greeting, "Buti naman ikakasal ka na, Stella. Mahigit trenta-anyos ka na nga diba?"

"Hello po." Stella gave him a slight nod but not responding to his baiting otherwise.

"Ang daming handa ng Daddy mo. Hinay-hinay sa pag-kain ha? Mahirap na. Baka tumaba ka ng sobra. Hindi ka na magkasya sa wedding gown mo," Tito Boy teased with a chuckle.

I grimaced. I knew it wasn't that he was trying to be a jerk. I happened to know that Tito Boy thought he was just being an upfront, honest, even helpful person. And while nothing he said was technically incorrect, it was more the manner with which he said the things that was often rude.

Stella shot him a suffering look but still didn't reply. She took Nick's arm and pulled him into the other room. And I wished I had an excuse to get away as well.

Tito Boy looked a little surprised but he went on, targeting Ate Roweena next. "Ikaw naman, Weena. Kelan ka ikakasal?"

My eyes lit up in alert and I noticed Ate Roweena's face pale while Lance shifted uncomfortably. I was going to say something but fortunately, my dad decided to reply first.

"Boy naman," Dad began. "Hinay-hinay lang. Hindi naman tayo nagmamadali."

Tito Boy chuckled again, tapping Ate Roweena's arm. "Biro lang naman, Weena," he resigned. "Pero mahuhuli na kayo. Taga-Forbes pa ang nabingwit ni Stella." He sounded impressed.

My mom was not. "Dating taga-dito lang din sa'tin yan," she relayed. "Ngayon lang big time na. Taga-Forbes na. Eh si Nicolas Batocabe lang naman yan. Bago nakahanap ng trabaho sa Dubai ang tatay n'ya at nakalipat sila." She gave Tito Boy a pointed look. "Alam mo ba nanligaw muna kay Rowena 'yan bago nakapag-pa-oo kay Stella?"

"Mommy!" Ate Roweena hissed.

"Tama naman. Pati nga kay Armi nanligaw si Nick, pagkatapos kay Rowena."

My eyes widened. "Mommy!" I complained even louder as Mom usually left that part of the narrative out of her stories as I guessed it wasn't as impressive as having gone after Ate Roweena. But I supposed tonight, unfortunately, my mom wanted to drive her point home for Tito Boy.

I thought I saw Lance laugh out of the corner of my eye but Ate Roweena finally decided to excuse themselves and walk away from the group, heading for the living-room-turned-dance-floor-complete-with-disco-ball in the next room.

Unfortunately for me, I had nothing else to occupy myself with. And I didn't want to keep tailing Stella and Nick all night. So all I could do was stand by in the fringes to watch the horrors unfold as Tito Boy acquainted himself with the rest of the crowd.

I managed to overhear several of Tito Boy's conversations with statements along the lines of—

"'Yung asawa ng anak ko si Mickey, buntis nanaman. Buti naman lalaki ulit."

"'Eh kaya ka nga nag-aasawa para magka-anak 'eh."

"Paano ka magkaka-boyfriend n'yan kung mataba ka?"

"Ikaw Martin, mamanahin mo na lang yung taxi ng Daddy mo?"

"Uy, si Will Salcedo ba 'yon?" Tito Boy suddenly called out as he narrowed his eyes, having spotted Will in the other room. "Hindi ko alam may importanteng bisita pala kayo dito. Baka kailangan nila ng magaling na contractor," he began, already plowing through the crowd eagerly to make his introductions.

"Tito Boy—!" I hissed, trying to call him back.

I already knew that Will didn't like to socialize with other people, let alone be accosted at a party to do business with someone he barely knew.

And of course, there was a very good chance that Tito Boy would say something annoying or inappropriate. Either way, I just knew it wasn't going to go down very well.

But I stopped short as Tito Boy had already caught up with Will, who looked surprised, if not slightly baffled at the sudden imposition.

On my way, I passed by Cattleya who had been, more or less like myself, simply watching all the exchanges and she gave me an airy, superior smirk. "Nice relatives, Armi."

I rolled my eyes, sighing.

IO

Kaibigan

It was another rainy afternoon and Martin had come to visit his "favorite sister" at work. And everyone knew what that was code for.

"Martin, ang dami mo nang utang sa'kin ha, please." I moved past him to clear Table 7 with my tray and always-handy *trapo*.

Martin made a pleading face at me. "Sige na, Ate," he coaxed. "Mababayaran kita this time talaga, pramis."

I shot him a surprised look. "Aba, at nakiki-'Ate' ka ata diyan ngayon," I remarked since Martin had basically stopped calling Ate Roweena and me 'Ate' as soon as he entered high school as though to indicate that he was all grown up.

Of course, he mostly used the term when he wanted to borrow money, which was too often. One time it was for a "school trip." Another time it was for "helping a friend" with a business venture that we were all pretty sure was actually a pyramid scheme. I usually never saw this money again and it was generally acknowledged in our family that lending Martin money was like giving to charity.

"Hindi nga," Martin insisted. "Kailangan ko lang ng pang-dagdag para sa YFC outing namin. May naipon na naman ako. Kulang nga lang. Sige na, Ate. Please?" He puckered up his face in a way that when he was five had looked cute, except I think he missed the memo that he was now freaking twenty-years old.

I groaned. "Dude, malapit na'ng matapos ang shift ko," I told him, trying to wipe Table 7 as efficiently as I could so I could clock out ASAP.

Martin's eyes lit up. "Ayos, pwede kang sumabay sa'min pauwi," he said, sounding eager to do me a favor.

I nodded absently. "Fine, pero kanya-kanyang pamasahe ha. May pinag-iipunan din ako 'no."

He shook his head. "May kotse yung kaibigan ko. He's going to Las Pinas today, so nag-offer siya na sumabay na lang din daw ako. Papunta na siya siguro dito now. Patapos lang din siya ng work." He went on, his eyes wide with enthusiasm. "This guy is so cool, Armi. He drives a Nissan Skyline. He went to Southridge. Na-meet ko rin siya sa YFC."

I narrowed my eyes at Martin in caution. Martin's friends from YFC were usually, and ironically, the dodgy kind.

"I'm sure magugustuhan mo rin siya. He's also into music," Martin relayed, his gaze distracting towards the restaurant's double doors as it opened. "Ayan na pala si George," he announced.

I stopped stacking plates for a second and looked up to follow Martin's gaze.

Okay. I didn't want to seem like a cliché, but seriously, when this guy tousled his hair to shake off the rain and then met my gaze with a smile, my jaw almost dropped.

This George was *super* F'ing cute. Like a less dopey-looking Coco Martin. He was wearing a black, long-sleeved *Slayer* t-shirt, faded jeans, and honest-to-gosh Doc Martens.

My alternative-indie heart skipped a beat.

George nodded in acknowledgment of the greeting, raising his hand in a brief wave at Martin as he walked up to us.

"Hiii..." I waved like an idiot.

Martin shot me the weirdest look ever then rolled his eyes.

Seriously, he should have known better.

But I shook off my earlier fluster and managed to remember who I was and everything as I shook his hand.

"—she's finishing work, pero sabi ko sabay na rin siya sa'tin pauwi," Martin was telling George.

George met my gaze again. "Sure," he replied with another smile. "Hey, baka gusto n'yong mag-merienda muna dito. My treat. Bagong sweldo tayo today," he beamed. "Also pancakes are like my super favorite food."

And I couldn't stop grinning.

"Kanan ka diyan sa susunod na traffic light." Martin gestured towards the front of the car as George drove us home.

"Don't worry. Malapit na." I rapped the back of the driver's seat from behind.

"Wala namang abala," George replied, glancing back at me.

I bit back my smile again and noticed Martin shake his head from the passenger seat.

George seemed like a pretty impressive person and it was obvious why Martin didn't want to share his attention. I knew he wished I made myself invisible and stayed quiet for the entire drive but George was the one who kept initiating conversations with me.

"My degree is Business Econ so medyo challenging to bring it to this local agricultural NGO but that's why they hired me. Para ma-improve yung systems nila."

"Wow." I looked over at Martin and put my hand on his shoulder. "Sabi pala ni Martin you're also into music?"

George smiled. "A, oo. Nag-gi-gitara din ako konti."

I honestly couldn't be more gobsmacked. "Really?"

Martin rolled his eyes again and somewhat in resignation, volunteered the information. "May banda sila Ate."

George flicked me an impressed look. "Talaga?"

I dismissed it with a wave, coloring slightly. "Wala lang naman. We do gigs sa mga small bars dito. We're called 'Anywhere/Anytime'," I supplied with a shrug.

George's eyes lit up. "What? Talaga? I think I've actually heard you guys once sa BF. You were pretty good," he praised. "I thought 'yung tunog n'yo was parang...'Orange and Lemons' or 'Hale' back in the day or something."

My jaw dropped in surprise and pleasure. "Wow! Salamat."

"Okay, we're here!" Martin announced, gesturing for George to pull over in front of our house.

George's car was a two-door boy-racer model so I was waiting for Martin to exit the car first so I could get out but George moved quickly, hopping out and pushing his seat forward instead before holding out his hand to help me.

I blinked at the uncommon gallantry. "Uh, thanks."

Martin was already at the gate, holding it open for me as though he was eager for us to get inside.

"Hey, baka you can show me some guitar tricks. Nandito ba'ng gitara mo?" George asked me, looking up at our house.

I shot him a questioning look. "Akala ko may lakad ka pa after this?"

He shrugged. "Pwede naman akong ma-late."

"Okay." I nodded readily as I stepped back towards the house. "Kunin ko lang sa loob." I gestured across the street. "Doon tayo sa chapel. Doon ako madalas mag-practice."

"Ayos." He smiled, shoving his hands in his pockets to wait with Martin outside our gate.

On my way back out, after having gotten my good guitar, I saw that Ate Roweena and Bingka with Basti were standing at the gate too.

It looked like my sisters were about to take Basti for his evening walk and George was kneeling down to pet the dog.

"Sama ka, Armi?" Ate Roweena prompted me.

"Ah, mag-gi-gitara lang kami ni George sandali sa chapel."

Ate Roweena narrowed her eyes at me suspiciously but I didn't indulge her. And before she could prod me any further, a noisy revving of another car that had just driven around the corner made us all look up. Basti barked out loud and tried to run onto the road but Ate Roweena held his leash firm.

It was an unfamiliar gold convertible sports car. But when it paused at the curb across the street, the passenger window rolled down and Lance waved at all of us from inside. "Hi guys," he greeted us all with a smile.

"Hi, Kuya Lance!" Bingka waved at him.

Lance smiled back at her before looking over at Ate Roweena. "We were just about to come over to see you."

We? I raised an eyebrow as the convertible top folded down to see that Will was actually driving the car. But he just looked at all of us silently, his face as stoic as ever as his gaze moved to meet mine.

Lance went on, still sitting in the car. "Just wanted to remind you guys about my birthday party on Saturday," he called out, shifting halfway up his seat as though in a motion to get out. "I'm getting this great DJ. It should be awesome."

"Maraming salamat nga pala ulit. For inviting all of us," Ate Roweena said, still smiling even as she tried to keep Basti from getting away.

"Ayos," Martin cheered. "Uy," he called out to Lance. "Si George nga pala, kaibigan ko." He gestured to him as George finally stood up. "Okay lang ba, sama rin siya sa party?"

As soon as Martin mentioned it, I noticed Will's gaze shift sharply.

"Martin," Ate Roweena hissed. "Hindi mo siya party."

But Lance shrugged, nodding amicably. "Um, oo naman. The more, the merrier."

"Nice." Martin turned to high-five George, who returned the high-five curtly even as he seemed to have also met and was holding Will's somber gaze.

Everyone else was preoccupied with either talking about Lance's party or tending the dog.

George gave Will a short nod in greeting. But Will just narrowed his eyes, almost imperceptibly, back at him.

My eyebrows furrowed as I observed the tense exchange

but only for a split second as Will clenched his jaw then looked away.

"Let's go," he told Lance.

Lance blinked in alert and slid back into his seat. "Um, okay. Hey, see you guys later!" He waved back at us again before Will revved the engine to drive away and within seconds, the car was gone.

Alam Na This

I sat on the brick planter bench at the chapel as I tried to show George some clumsy fretting on my guitar.

I was like the last person in the world who would be able to make friends so fast but George had a very down-to-earth, approachable personality. He had an amazing way of making anyone feel at ease around him.

"Teka, teka." I was laughing as I made a mistake on the chord. "Ilang buwan ko na pina-practice 'to 'eh."

But he simply laughed with me. "Relax ka lang. Ako lang naman ang audience. Don't worry, mababa lang ang standards ko," he joked.

"Aha, ganoon pala ha?" I smacked his arm, feigning offense. "Salbahe ka."

He chuckled again. "Ikaw naman. Joke lang shempre."

I shook my head in mirth and handed him the guitar.

"Sige nga, ikaw muna ulit. Ang daya naman kasi, mas malaki kamay mo kaysa sa'kin."

"Sure, kaya pala," he quipped, bending his head down to strum a few chords, his hair falling partway in his eyes. He had the longest eyelashes everrr…

I blinked to snap myself out of it and stop staring at him, racking my brain to occupy my thoughts with something else. "Hey. So," I began casually after a moment. "Pupunta ka nga sa party ni Lance?"

George looked up and paused to think. "Siguro," he replied, his expression vague. "Gaano katagal na sila nakatira dito?"

"Mga ilang buwan na." I gave him a curious look. "Magkakilala ba kayo?"

"Ni Lance? No."

"So…ni Will?" I prompted cautiously as from their earlier exchange clearly, there was something going on between them.

He looked at me as if considering his response before he looked away. "Actually, yeah," he relayed. "*Actually*…magkababata kami ni Will."

My eyes popped wide open in surprise. "Ha?"

He cracked a smirk, meeting my gaze again. "Weird ba? Given his reaction earlier, parang hindi kapani-paniwala, 'no?"

"Um, yeah, parang napansin ko nga." I pursed my lips, trying to suppress my inner *chismosa* but given the circumstances, the information seemed too juicy not to prod further. "May…nangyari ba sa inyo?"

George put my guitar down on his lap and looked around.

I figured he was about to tell me something embarrassing and he didn't want anyone else around to hear. I leaned forward in my seat.

"Driver ng family ni Will yung dad ko ever since bata pa ako. Doon na ako lumaki," he began. "Parang pamilya yung trato nila sa'min. Malaki ang tulong nila, lalo na sa school, for my scholarships. And when I graduated, Will's dad gave me a job at their company. Si Mr. Salcedo, mabait 'yun," he remarked with a wistful smile. "Parang anak din 'yung trato niya sa'kin."

His expression changed. "Tapos isang araw, mayroon akong ginawang proposal. I basically discovered that if we created a new operating level, it would improve our department's efficiency. And if I was assigned head of this new team, I would get a promotion. I would have had an opportunity to lead my own team for my initiative and build a wider network of contacts. Not to mention, mas makakatulong ako sa mom ko. Lalo na't wala na si Dad."

I was almost on the edge of my seat in suspense, listening to his story. "Tapos?"

George gave me a look and a sigh. "Tapos." He pursed his lips. "Will was asked to review the proposal and oversee the creation of the new team." He shrugged, seeming at a loss. "Siguro hindi niya nagustuhan or he didn't agree with my approach. So he promoted someone else to lead."

My eyes widened in shock. "What?"

"If you ask me, na-inggit lang siya kasi it was in his department that I had found na kulang yung operating levels. I guess he thought he was so perfect na hindi siya pwedeng magkamali." He sighed again. "But you know, they offered to keep me on. Demoted position nga lang."

My head was spinning. "B-but the department wouldn't even exist kung hindi mo naisip eh!" I sputtered in disbelief.

"Mm-hm." He swallowed as though he was having difficulty to go on with his story. "So I wasn't about to be humiliated simply for Will's amusement. Nag-resign na lang ako." He shook his head in derision. "Tapos ngayon, parang siya pa ang galit sa'kin," he huffed. "Well, kung ayaw niya ako makita, pumikit na lang siya."

My head was in my hands as I made a face in distaste. "I can't believe it." I shook my head. "Ever since talaga, I knew it! Napaka-arogante ng taong 'yan."

George made a big show of shrugging. "Tayong dalawa lang ang nakakakita ng tunay niyang kulay. Everybody else sure caters to his every whim."

I wrinkled my nose, nodding in agreement as I looked at George in sympathy. *Ay, grabe...*

"Ay, grabe," Ate Roweena commented, her eyes the widest I'd ever seen them. "Totoo nga?"

We were getting ready for Lance's party that weekend and I had just relayed the backstory about George and Will.

I tilted my head to regard her with a look. "Ate, come on."

"Parang hindi ako makapaniwala," Ate Roweena mused as she tried her best to straighten her wayward curly hair with a big brush. "Baka naman may ibang reason. Ang sama naman kung ginawa n'ya 'yon para lang mag-malaki. It seems very unethical. Not to mention unprofessional."

"Sino ba'ng pinag-uusapan natin?" I supplied, almost in ridicule. "Nakakagulat pa ba 'yun? Maski ang buong barangay alam na may sa demonyo siya 'no."

Ate Roweena pursed her lips, still shaking her head as though unable to fully absorb the news.

I turned back to check my minimal make-up in the mirror and didn't say anything more.

"Tatanungin ko si Lance mamaya," she spoke up. "Siguro naman alam n'ya ano talaga nangyari."

I rolled my eyes. "Please. Si Will nga ang ipag-explain mo. Siya kaya ang may sala. Either way, sana hindi ko siya makita sa party mamaya."

"Ang malas naman ni George."

"Ewan ko na lang ha," I remarked. "Mas malas ang mga taong walang modo."

"Ate! Ate!" Bingka burst into our room. She was followed by our frowning mom who was endeavoring to touch up the hairdo on our super *likot bunso*.

Mom stopped to blink at me. "Carmina, bakit puro itim ang suot mo? Hindi tayo pupunta sa lamay."

I resisted the urge to shake my head but as usual, before I could even formulate a response, she charged on, turning her attention to my sister.

"Rowena, magsuot ka ng alahas." Mom was looking Ate Roweena up and down. "Baka kung ano ang isipin nila. Dapat magustuhan ka ng mga magulang ni Lance. Gusto mo bang hiramin yung kwintas ko? Totoong gold 'yun. Galing Saudi." She gestured to the door, already making a move to fetch it even before my sister could respond.

Bingka twirled around in her short denim jumper dress, beaming up at us. "Kasing ganda n'yo na po ba ako, mga Ate?"

"Siyempre mas maganda pa," Ate Roweena replied with a wink and I watched as she bent down to adjust Bingka's fake pearl-encrusted headband.

I almost envied Bingka's enthusiasm. At her age, it almost didn't matter what you wore and nobody would judge you.

I on the other hand had to use some of my hard-earned money on an entirely new blouse just for this party since I figured my go-to 'Billie Eilish'-esque *lakwatsa* outfit would not be acceptable.

My mom came back into the room, proceeding to put a gold chain around Ate Roweena's neck. "Ayan," she said, looking pleased as she fluffed her daughter's hair about.

"Mommy," Ate Roweena began patiently. "Na-meet ko na 'yung mom ni Lance, remember? Mabait naman sila."

"Gusto ko lang naman makita nila kung gaano ka-bait at ka-ganda ang mga anak ko," Mom said, looking at each of us in turn with a smile. She put a hand on Ate Roweena's cheek then tilted her head in a prompt. "O siya, tara na." She beckoned us all out of the room, bending down to pick up something by the hallway as she went along.

I glanced down, narrowing my eyes. "Mommy, tatawid lang tayo ng kalsada, hindi sasakay ng barko," I reminded, gesturing to her inappropriately-sized knockoff Louis Vuitton handbag. "Hindi n'yo kailangan ng maleta."

She gave me a purely authoritative look like she didn't know how I could ever doubt her knowledge in these matters. "Aba, eh kung may kapareho tayo ng suot na damit? Or madumihan yung damit ko? Kailangan may costume change na nakahanda."

She waved over Martin who had been waiting on the couch, playing on his phone. "Halika na, Martin. Rene," she called to my dad.

Dad was sitting at the dining table behind his newspaper. He looked almost surprised that having him come along to the party was not in fact a joke.

"Mag-ayos kayo ng mga sarili n'yo," Mom nagged on.

Nevertheless, my dad stood up, bedgrudgingly putting his paper down. "Hindi ba birthday party lang naman ang pupuntahan natin?" he commented in ridicule as our mom rushed us all out the door. "Bakit parang bibisita tayo ng palasyo?"

And Ate Roweena and I laughed.

12

Crazy. Rich.

Walking up the driveway to the party, the house at 214 San Antonio Avenue looked less like a resort like last time and more like the elegant mansion it was.

It appeared that the majority of the renovations had been completed. The big trees lining the driveway had been decorated with pearl *capiz* and colorful bamboo lamps and the house glowed a magnificent yellow in the dark.

The driveway, as well as the street front, were full of fancy parked cars. I was no Math genius but it looked like Lance was hosting a birthday party attended by at least two hundred guests.

Mom and Bingka led the way as our family went up the front porch to step into the house.

Lance was already beaming as he ran up to meet us by the foyer. He took Ate Roweena's hand and gestured to the rest of us. "Welcome po! Come in. My mom would love to meet you."

As Lance led us further into the house, the cool breeze of airconditioning hit me, the unmistakable delicious aroma of fried food mixed with something probably produced by Glade, soft jazz music coming through the built-in speaker system throughout the house, and the ambient hum of the two hundred guests chattering daintily among themselves.

I noticed Martin ducking away and disappearing into the party crowd.

Dad watched Martin leave, looking like he wanted to do the exact same thing but Mom grabbed his arm.

"Magpakilala lang muna tayo sa mga magulang ni Lance, okay?" Mom hissed. "Pagkatapos n'un, kung gusto mo, umuwi ka na."

Dad merely grimaced in response.

I chuckled and took the opportunity to slip away myself as I was sure it was in nobody's best interest that I was introduced to Lance's parents.

Anyway, I was already craning my neck to search the crowd as George had made it clear in a few of our text exchanges over the past week that he was looking forward to hanging out with me at the party. I had to admit I was a bit excited to see him again.

Not counting the blip that was Nick Batocabe, I had to say I was no slouch at drawing in the random *manliligaw*. Of course, not like Ate Roweena. But I had it on good authority that more guys would have tried if my resting bitch face hadn't scared them away.

In any case, I was more often the one doing the rejecting

rather than being rejected. But lately, it was getting more and more difficult to even meet any suitable or, even in the least, interesting guys, impressive or otherwise. Suffice it to say, I hadn't had a crush like George in a long while.

Across one of the large dining rooms, I spotted Stella standing by one of several professionally catered buffet tables. The setup looked like a hotel breakfast station with labels in front of the food platters covered with shiny metal lids and burners underneath to keep the food warm. There was even a guy setting up a crepe station for dessert.

Stella's eyes lit up when she met my gaze as I approached her. "Armi, uy!" She motioned up the front of the room where my parents, Ate Roweena, and Bingka were being presented to who must be Lance's mom among a group of elegantly-dressed women. "Ano 'yan, namamanhikan na?" she wanted to know, already chomping on a chicken skin *chicharon* she picked up from the *pica pica* selection.

I hissed in disbelief. "Ang bilis mo naman, pare."

"Come *on*," Stella wailed, her eyes pinned on the scene across the room. "Tignan mo 'yan si Weena," she began. "Ni hindi pa tabihan si Lance. Hindi pa ba obvious na sila na?"

I watched Ate Roweena fidget uncomfortably during the formalities and furrowed my eyebrows. "Alam mo naman na mahiyain 'yan si Ate 'eh."

"Wushu," Stella hooted. "Hindi na uso magpakipot. Sung-gab na!" she cheered with such conviction, I couldn't help but laugh.

Nick popped up just then and touched Stella's arm. "Babe, they're serving dinner na daw. Hey, Armi," he greeted upon seeing me. "Tara, hanap tayo ng table sa labas." He beckoned the two of us to follow him. But not before pausing to gesture towards a big painting mounted on the wall we were passing. "Did you notice all the artwork Lance's parents put up in the house? I noticed they have a Rene Alba framed print. You know, Tita has an original Rene Alba. I think it costs over nine million pesos."

***

I slumped back in my chair after dinner, staring at my silent phone. *Minsan lang. Minsan lang talaga. Bakit ba hindi ako swertehin kahit minsan lang?* I thought to myself with a frown.

George was still a no-show.

I craned my neck to canvas the party again, around the dining tables set up in the garden and surveying up the stairs through the doors into the house but all I could see were a bunch of preppy guys dressed almost exactly like Lance.

Nick was talking with a small group of people near the garden's two-tier waterfall and log fountain water feature while Stella was still sitting with me at our table, polishing off the last of her pandan dessert.

Admittedly, I was still holding on to hope that George would make a fashionably late entrance. That was until I spotted Martin from across the lawn ambling over, his head bowed as he read something from his own phone which he announced as he got closer.

"Hindi daw makakapunta si George."

My face fell. "Ay, bakit daw?"

"Busy," was Martin's short response before he promptly turned to leave.

I made a face. It was quite disappointing. Not to mention, I wouldn't have gone through all the trouble to look actually presentable tonight had I known he wouldn't be here.

As Martin headed away, he walked past Ate Roweena walking towards us just as Stella spoke up beside me. "George? 'Yan ba 'yung sinabi mong cute guy? Hindi siya dadating?"

And Ate Roweena overheard. "Ay, hindi dadating si George?" She regarded me with a suspicious look as she slid into the empty seat on my other side to whisper hoarsely, "Sa tingin mo dahil nandito si Will?"

I blew out a breath. "Ay, I wouldn't be surprised."

"Tinanong ko si Lance," Ate Roweena started with a conspiratorial look. "'Yung hindi obvious na tanong naman siyempre—"

Stella leaned closer. "Uy, this sounds like chismis. Game."

"Na-kwento ko na sa'yo, Stella," I told her.

Her eyes lit up in recognition. "Ah, siya rin ba 'yung guy na hindi natanggap for promotion."

"Yuh."

"Well," Ate Roweena continued. "Hindi daw alam ni Lance ang lahat pero kung ano man daw ang nangyari sigurado daw siya na hindi si Will ang mali."

I rolled my eyes. "*Char.* Siyempre 'yun ang sasabihin ni Lance."

Stella's forehead was creased. "Look, guys, I promise," she began. "Will is a really nice guy. Ilang lang talaga siya sa strangers."

I waved her away, slightly annoyed. "Oh god, please, Stella. Hayaan mo na lang na isumpa namin siya hanggang kamatayan forever."

Just then, the distinctive opening beats by Dua Lipa floated out from the open patio doors and Nick swooned out loud from across the lawn. "Oh! I love this song. Stella, it's our song!" He called out. "We have to dance." He hurried over to tug Stella away with a short, "See you later, Armi, Weena."

"Tara!" Ate Roweena had a big smile too as she grabbed my hand and dragged me towards the house to follow.

I had to blink to adjust my eyesight since while the garden area was fully lit with basketball stadium-grade lights, the lighting inside the main lounge of the house had been dimmed and the floor cleared for the unavoidable disco.

I gave my sister a half-hearted smile as I did my usual two-step on the dance floor while she and Stella did full-on *Living Room Routine.*

Ate Roweena motioned her finger at me, mouthing *Come on!* but she shook her head with a sly smile knowing full well I never shined my best on the dance floor.

I was in fact relieved—possibly grateful—when Lance appeared out of nowhere, took Ate Roweena's hand, and took over dancing with her for me. I watched the two happy couples dance to the *doof doof* dubstep remix, cracking a smile in spite of myself as I made my hasty retreat.

When I backed up, I bumped into someone.

13

Ang Sayaw atbp.

"Oops, sorry." I whirled around to apologize automatically and my eyes widened.

It was Will.

He looked at me for a moment. "It's fine."

I stepped back.

It appeared Will Salcedo had found his "sungit spot" in one isolated corner of the open plan lounge at the billiards table. It was adjacent to the darkened dance floor but it was lit overhead by a single fluorescent bulb.

I actually thought it was the perfect spot for him since it kept him technically in the middle of the party but it was secluded enough that anyone passing by would easily be able to tell the space was absolutely not for casual socializing.

I regarded him with an already mocking look.

He was bent over the fuzzy green table, lining up his shot. There were no other cue sticks lying around and even as a few other people were lingering in the fringes, watching him play, it was clear that he wasn't going to invite them to join him.

"Are you winning?" I couldn't help but ask. It was a sarcastic question since obviously, he wasn't playing against anyone but he didn't look fazed.

"Marunong ka?"

"Siyempre."

He straightened up and held the cue stick in his hand out to me.

I blinked in surprise. "Um. Okay." I walked up to take it from him.

Will walked over to the cabinet in the back to get a second cue stick. "Solids?"

"Fine. Stripes."

I almost wanted to call out the efficient way he moved around the table to rack all the balls up. That was before without further ado, he proceeded to break. I supposed he wasn't familiar with "ladies first."

Honestly, I didn't know why I was still surprised. And given all the incriminating things I knew about him, I also didn't know why I didn't just come up with an excuse—any excuse—to go *anywhere else* instead.

I happened to glance back at the dance floor to see Stella making wide dancing gestures with her two thumbs up *at me* and I could tell even over the music that she was howling in full support of what she must have thought she was seeing going on over here.

I had to shake my head in ridicule and simply turned back to watch Will and wait for my turn. I figured Stella had conveniently forgotten that I'd said I was going to loathe Will

Salcedo for the rest of eternity and that if I had *literally* any-thing else to do, I wouldn't even be here in the first place.

Besides, the feeling was obviously mutual. Will wasn't saying anything. He wouldn't even look at me.

Tonight, he was wearing jeans and a button-down, long-sleeved collared shirt with the sleeves folded up his forearms. It was a more casual look than I was used to seeing him in, not that it made him look any less hot—*este*, evil! I meant *evil*.

In any case, when it was my turn, I walked up to the table and sunk two easy balls into the side pockets before missing my next shot. I stepped aside to gesture Will to have a go.

Each of us took one more turn in absolute silence before I couldn't help myself again. "So hindi ka talaga makikipag-usap?" I prompted wryly, picking up the *tisa* to chalk up the tip of my cue stick.

He assessed the arrangement of the balls, still not looking at me. "Anong gusto mong sabihin ko?"

I made a big show of shrugging, holding up the *tisa*. "Um," I began and gestured around, offhand. "Ang daming tao sa party 'no? Kilala kaya talaga ni Lance silang lahat?"

"Well, I certainly don't," was all he said before bending down to take his shot.

Okay... I wasn't about to carry the entire conversation all by myself. "I suppose pwede naman tahimik lang tayo for the whole game. Hindi talaga 'yon weird." I walked around the table to line up my next shot. I glanced up at him so he would move over. "Excuse me."

He brushed past behind me on his way to get the *tisa* and after my shot, he strolled over to take his turn. He bent down to sink two consecutive balls in the corner pocket, finishing and straightening up before he even spoke again. "I didn't think you were the 'small talk' kind of person."

Like me. I almost thought I heard the rest of his statement in my head but I shook it off despite his perceptiveness.

"Sure," I agreed, moving along the table to find a good position then sinking a red-striped ball in the pocket before going on to rationalize. "Pero may difference naman yung iwas 'small talk' and straight-up being unsociable."

I came over to his side again, leaning down to line up my next shot but the balls weren't quite in the right spots so I decided instead to hide some solids. I nodded to myself, satisfied with my strategy.

He glanced down at me. "Depends anong ibig mong sabihin by unsociable. Madalas societal norms require an un-necessary level of disingenuousness."

"Okay..." I remarked as I straightened up, mystified at his stubborn logic. "Eh kung ganyan ka lagi magsalita, talagang walang makikipag-kaibigan sa'yo." I watched him furrow his eyebrows in concentration to pull off a particularly tricky shot as he leaned over the table beside me.

"I don't make friends easily," he replied, his shot making a loud *thunk* as the white ball hit its mark dead-on. "Besides, making new friends is overrated."

I smirked, already expecting his short response. It struck me just how different being around Will was from being around George. Having a conversation with Will was like try-ing to squeeze out the last bits of toothpaste from the tube.

Tedious. Excruciating.

He straightened up to study the table again before walking around and his gaze narrowed. I could almost see the wheels spinning in his head as he tried to figure out how to get his solid ball out from behind one of my striped ones.

Against my better judgment and partly because I was curious how Will would react in the face of hard truths, I couldn't help but highlight this disparity. "I know some people who make friends easily. In fact, kaka-meet ko lang sa kanya last week."

That made Will's head snap up to meet my gaze and he missed his shot. He paused as if either in an effort to measure my tone or to calculate his response but his expression remained bland. "Well...I suppose actually madali lang pala makipag-kaibigan," he amended, his voice calm. "Ang tanong is if he can keep them."

I almost chuckled in incredulity. "Wow..." I drawled, my eyebrows raised as I walked up to take my turn. "Talagang may issues kayo ni George 'no? Wala nang bawian?"

"Bakit ba gusto mong malaman?" His expression had a tinge of annoyance in it.

I pursed my lips. I was by no means intimidated by his question but I didn't want to start an argument or make a scene in the middle of the party so I made my next statement in caution. "Just trying to gauge kung gaano ka ka-bitter, wondering how you have any friends at all." I bent down to line up my shot. "Apparently, iba-iba ang impressions ng mga tao sa'yo. Hindi ko talaga gets." I shook my head and punctuated my sentence with a rebound shot off the side of the table.

Will merely gave me a strange scrutinizing look. It was a long look.

I returned the stare, undaunted. I had to think real hard to remember if I had actually ever even seen him smile before. He was always so composed, sedate. There was also no hint of reaction on his face regarding the fact that I was kicking his ass in the billiards game.

He didn't offer any response to my statement.

I blew out an exasperated breath before leaning over the table. "Eight ball, corner pocket."

We both watched the ball roll neatly into the hole.

I glanced up to meet his gaze and when he said nothing more, I just shrugged again. Then I lay the cue stick on the table and walked away.

14

Bad trip

sorry last min work thing. c u—

I swiped George's message away nonchalantly, pocketing my phone as I walked through an archway in Lance's big house, heading away from the disco lounge, towards the quieter, more brightly lit part of the house where the older people were gathered.

Two uniformed servers were walking around with trays of coffees and sparkling glasses of wine. A professional pianist was playing soft classical music on the smaller piano in the corner.

I was intending to approach one of the servers to grab a cup of coffee when I spotted my youngest sister past a small crowd by the piano. She was gaily performing her favorite song and dance number in front of the other moms.

Unfortunately, Bingka's current repertoire she'd picked up

from TikTok. It wasn't particularly delicate and happened to include the infamous "twerk" move.

I observed the amused gazes of her audience. I was not under any illusion that even one of them found Bingka's particular number enchanting and possibly the least bit appropriate for an eleven-year-old.

I recognized my mother's voice easily, not just because it dominated over the hushed chatter that she was drawing other people's critical stares but also because she said, "Nakita n'yo ba? Dalawang chandelier!"

Mom was across the room, sitting at one of the tables and talking to three other women. "Ah, 'yung bunso ko, malapit na siya mag-graduate ng Grade 6," she was saying as if in response to someone's question as she gestured to Bingka. "Napaka-masayahin at napaka-bait na bata. Mana talaga sa nanay."

I couldn't hear what the other women were saying but unfortunately, my mother's next statement was, "Pangarap ko talaga na pag-laki niya makapag-asawa rin siya ng mabuti tulad ng panganay ko si Rowena. Nakita n'yo ba, in-love na in-love si Lance sa kanya? At pagkatapos ng kasal, siguradong may mga mayayamang kaibigan din si Lance na pwede niya ipakilala sa mga ibang anak ko."

I grimaced, doing an immediate about-face to head away from there. I passed the dance floor again on my way out to the gardens just as Nick and Stella were stepping back to head for the refreshments table and Stella noticed the look on my face.

"Dude, okay ka lang?" she asked, pulling away from Nick for a moment to stop me by the door.

I grabbed her arm, groaning under my breath. "Ugh. Bakit ba parang laging nananadya talagang ipahiya kaming lahat ng pamilya ko?"

Stella stifled her mirth behind her hand. Then she elbowed me, motioning her mouth toward the dance floor again. "At least hindi napapansin ni Lance," she pointed out and I followed her gaze.

Ate Roweena and Lance were now dancing with a small group of other people and Lance was looking adoringly at Ate Roweena as she laughed at something one of their other friends said. She nudged another guy's shoulder playfully before Lance took her hand again.

That made me smile, at least in relief that Stella was probably right. I was confident that Lance had gotten to know our mother well enough in the last few months and if that, on top of everything, wasn't enough to scare him off, then it was likely that nothing could.

Out of the corner of my eye, I spotted Martin with a group of guys near the pool past the gardens outside and something about the way they were huddled together seemed distinctly suspicious. I bid Stella a 'see you later' before stepping out of the house to head towards him.

As I came closer, I wrinkled my nose as I could swear I faintly smelled something. "Ano 'yun?"

Martin's eyes lit up in alarm upon seeing me approach but he was biting his lip to keep from laughing even though his other friends were already cackling raucously, roughhousing, and pushing each other around.

I tugged my brother's arm to pull him away from the group for a second and I narrowed my eyes at him. "Hoy, Martin,"

I began with a stern tone. "Anong ginagawa n'yo, ha? Wala kayo sa park. Bahay ng ibang tao 'to."

He nudged me, a wry grin on his face. "Ate naman," he cajoled.

"Ano 'yung naaamoy ko?" I wanted to know, giving him a wary look.

"Ah, wala 'yon." He waved to dismiss me before relaying a joke, gesturing to a big guy wearing a 'Punks Not Dead' t-shirt. "Eto kasi si Bruno, naputulan nanaman daw sila ng tubig. Last week pa hindi naliligo, parang sira—"

There was a loud yell and a sudden splash and on instinct, I jumped away, narrowly avoiding the spray of water as one of Martin's friends fell into the pool.

A wave of water splattered onto the pebbled pavement. The rest of Martin's crowd burst out laughing again even as some of them had wet splotches on their clothes. Meanwhile, their friend flailed around in the deep end of the pool, splashing some more.

I looked around the area as quite a few guests were looking on in distaste and whispering among themselves.

I pursed my lips and when I turned back to Martin with my look of disapproval, he at least stopped laughing and looked sheepish.

But all I could do was shake my head in exasperation and walk away.

On my way back into the house, I happened to pass a group of girls standing by the fountain, almost accosted by the overpowering whiff of their combined floral perfume scents and as luck would have it, Cattleya was among them.

I lowered my eyes to avoid meeting her gaze but she didn't even see me.

I heard her though.

"You should have heard the loud-mouthed crass opinions of their Tito Boy at Stella's engagement party," Cattleya was going on. "It's like the entire family was raised sa tabi ng riles."

I winced, closing my eyes in horror.

It was like it wasn't enough that Tito Boy was an opinionated jerk and my mom, a tactless brag, but my brother also had to be an unruly junkie.

I wished my dad had at least stuck around long enough to rein in the madness even a little bit but he had probably already gone home, unable to stand the party chaos himself.

I moved again to leave and was almost through the door into the house when I overheard something else I wish I hadn't.

"Seriously. Lance must be out of his mind. I've always hoped he would get together with Monica, you know, Will's famous sister? Diba mas bagay? *Sobra.*"

****

15

Bad news

"Paano ba 'yan, Mommy? Bakit hindi magbukas na lang tayo ng internet café? Pareho lang din naman ang itsura ng sala natin eh."

I looked up from my phone at the sound of my dad's wry announcement as he paused at the doorway of our living room and I glanced around.

Ate Roweena was seated next to me on the couch, her head bent down over her old flip phone with a frown. Martin was sitting in the rattan rocking chair, holding his phone with two hands, playing one of his louder zombie shooting games while Basti slept by his feet. Bingka was stretched out on the rug on the floor with her light-up pink cat head-phones on, absorbed in watching a kid's show on YouTube on a much-used iPad she had won from a raffle three years ago. Two electric fans on either side of the living room were running full blast in an attempt to counter the heat wave. It was pretty much a typical weekend mid-afternoon scenario in our household.

Dad met my smirk with one of his own before he disappeared back through the hallway with only a shake of his head.

The rest of my siblings had barely noticed the brief interruption, not even looking up from any of their various devices.

Ate Roweena let out a huge frustrated sigh beside me and I looked over. "Ano yan?"

She was still frowning over her phone but she tried to dismiss me with an offhand wave. "Ah, wala lang. Hindi nanaman kasi nag-re-reply si Lance."

I raised my eyebrows to repeat, "Nanaman?"

"Diba na-kwento ko sa'yo na ma-a-assign ako sa training sa Makati for six weeks?" she relayed. "Malapit siya sa BTI tower so sabi ko mag-lunch out sana kami this week." She sighed again and put her phone down. "Pero super busy siya siguro."

I was aware that Lance had told Ate Roweena that he and Cattleya were going back to stay at their condo for a while to take care of some business. But that had been well over two weeks ago. I tried to think back. I couldn't even recall that they had seen each other since Lance's birthday party. "Kailan nga daw pala sila babalik dito?"

She fidgeted in her seat as she replied, "Hindi daw niya alam."

"Hindi niya alam?" I echoed, making a face. "Ang labo naman. Paano naman na hindi niya alam? Baka naman iba lang ang pagkaintindi mo."

She thrust her phone at me. "Ayan o, tignan mo."

I watched her face warily as I took the phone, smoothing back the scotch tape, the only thing holding the battery on, before reading.

Ate Roweena's expression seemed neutral but she had to be feeling anxious. If I was her, I certainly would be. Lance's behavior had all the telltale signs of "ghosting." Only I was sure Lance wasn't that kind of guy. I was convinced he could never be such a jerk and do that to my sister. But I bit my lip as I scrolled through her messages.

A particular one from Cattleya that stood out made me frown even more.

"*Monica's a little nervous about her quarter exams and I want to be around for encouragement. What better source of moral support than your family, right? Wink. Wink,*" I read aloud, my tone as dull as she sounded in my head. "'Encouragement' is misspelled and 'family' is all caps. Nice." I rolled my eyes, an inkling of suspicion forming in my mind recalling Cattleya's comment at Lance's party regarding whom she thought was the better match for her brother.

Ate Roweena shrugged. "Ang galing talaga ni Monica 'no? I guess tama nga naman if you look at it that way."

I grimaced, almost feeling her pain as I noted Ate Roweena's carefully disguised dejected expression but before I could formulate any words of reassurance—

"Wala, pinagpalit ka na ng syota mo," Martin jeered even as he didn't look up from his phone.

"Martin!" I hissed my scolding, launching a throw pillow in his face but he managed to block it with his hand as he laughed. The pillow fell to the floor and Basti pounced on it with a playful growl.

Ate Roweena shook her head in mirth before sighing yet again. "Either way, sana deretso na lang nila sabihin sa'kin. Maiintindihan ko naman kung mas gusto ni Lance si Monica eh."

I smacked her arm. "Ano ba'ng pinagsasabi mo? Obvious kaya na ikaw ang gusto ni Lance 'no. Maski sinong tanungin mo dito sa barangay na nakakita sa inyong dalawa alam 'yon." I puffed my chest out. "Hayaan mo nga 'yan si Cattleya, sinungaling. Siguradong busy lang naman si Lance. Tignan mo, mag-re-reply din 'yan maya-maya."

Ate Roweena took her phone back, only a non-committal expression on her face before she turned back to me to change the subject. "Kamusta pala si George? Nagkikita pa ba kayo?"

I shook my head carelessly. "May inaasikaso yata siya sa kliyente nila sa Quezon City so hindi siya napapadaan dito sa south lately."

"May nililigawan 'yon sa QC," Martin supplied out loud. "Ipinagpalit ka na rin."

"Aww, Armi!" Ate Roweena flashed me a deeply crestfallen consoling look.

But I just chuckled. I myself had seen the handful of "couple selfies" with a *mestiza* girl that George had posted on his social media.

I supposed I was a little disappointed with the whole George situation but I also had to admit that it was more likely the thrill of someone new that had appealed to me more than George himself.

Still, he was as interesting as any friend I'd had so when George texted that he would try to come around next week to hang out, I'd sent a friendly reply, already resigned it was better not to get my hopes up regardless.

My dad reappeared in the hallway with a clatter and he came back into the living room, followed by our mom.

Mom bent down to Bingka first to put her hand on her shoulder. "Bingka, anak," she started, "doon ka muna manood sa kwarto. Kailangan namin kausapin ng Daddy ang mga ate at kuya mo."

Bingka looked up at her before instantly nodding. "Opo, Mommy."

Ate Roweena's eyes had lit up in slight recognition and she shifted in her seat but she didn't say anything.

I narrowed my eyes, looking around at everyone as only Martin and I seemed surprised by the unexpected family meeting. But I had to give props to my brother's sense of self-preservation as the moment my mom sat down on the other couch seat across from us, Martin popped out of the rocking chair, startling the idling dog before he dashed through the kitchen and out the back door.

"Oy, Martin!" Mom called out but she was only able to partly yell out "Ikaw susunod," before Martin disappeared, the door rattling behind him.

I turned back to my sister then glanced up at my dad. "Susunod saan?" But neither of them replied and I watched Basti patter on the floor to approach Ate Roweena's leg to continue snoozing before I met my mom's no-nonsense gaze again in expectation.

Unfortunately, Mom said pretty much what I had already been expecting them to tell us these last few months since

I'd overheard her and Dad's conversation at Stella's engagement party.

About the money.

In particular, that we didn't have any.

And a proposal about how we might be able to make ends meet if everyone made just a few little sacrifices.

And by everyone, she meant me.

My eyes popped open. "Ano po? At saan?"

"Sa construction company ni Tito Boy sa Cavite," Mom relayed. "Kailangan nila ng bagong receptionist sa opisina. Mondays to Saturdays."

After a short pause, her expression changed. "Dapat nga magpasalamat tayo na may trabahong in-offer si Tito Boy para hindi ka na mahihirapan pa'ng maghanap," she added, her eyebrow raised in an indication that she wasn't accepting any protests or complaints.

But I had to ask. "Pati po Sabado? Mauubos po ang oras ko kaka-commute. Saka may practice po 'yung banda namin tuwing Sabado."

Mom tilted her head, her gaze steady on me. "Ipagpaliban mo na muna 'yang banda mo, Carmina," she instructed. "Mas importante makapagbayad tayo ng utang. Mabuti nga maayos na trabaho 'yan eh at sigurado ang sahod mo. Kami rin ng Daddy at Ate mo mag-da-dagdag ng trabaho para makabawi tayo kaagad."

I pursed my lips and looked over at Ate Roweena who merely gave me a shrug.

She couldn't help me. She was already doing her share, probably even more than her share.

I knew it was partly my fault for not making enough of an effort to find a better job but I couldn't express emphatically enough how much I would dislike working for our obnoxious Tito Boy. And I definitely didn't want to get stuck working there forever.

"Hangga't makabayad lang naman tayo ng utang, diba Mommy? Mga three months? Six months?" I almost dreaded her answer.

Mom stifled a moan. "Pagkatapos, ano? Babalik ka sa Pancake House part-time?" she mocked then turned to my dad. "Rene, pagsabihan mo nga 'yang anak mo, ha? Hindi pwedeng sarili lang ang iniisip natin, lalo na sa mga panahon na'to."

Dad looked anxiously back and forth between me and Mom before he met my gaze again, his wrinkled face looking ever more haggard. "Sige na, Armi," he complied, earning him Mom's quick dagger look of disbelief but he tried to avoid it as he went on to speak to me. "Sabihin natin na pansamantala lang ito. Anim na buwan lang muna at hangga't may makita kang mas regular na trabaho."

Mom huffed in displeasure and I could already tell what was running through her head about how Dad always let me get away with murder but she looked back at me to give me a stern prompting look.

Negotiation time was over. This was the best deal I was going to get.

My frown deepened but all I could do was nod. "Opo."

***

16

Intermission

"At wala sa bass, mga kaibigan, palakpakan po natin ang aming napaka-late na miyembro, in-abandona na kami—ayun o, si Miss Armi Benitez!"

I'd already twisted my face in a grimace as I walked into our usual bar hangout, making my way down the darkened aisle between the crowd and the tables through the dimly lit outdoor dining area amidst the smattering of applause.

I simply raised my hand to point a finger in acknowledgment directly at the stage where Boboy and our band had just finished up their set without me.

I could barely hear anything else over the noise. It would have been a typical Saturday night. Except for the big tarp hanging on the wall behind the stage, a spray-painted banner that said '*Boo! Closing Down Party!*' So there were more people in the place than normal.

"Ayos! Kami po ang Anywhere/Anytime. Magandang gabi!"

Boboy bid the audience as the guys played the last chords of a covered Typecast song.

More applause.

I slid onto a bench seat at one of the tables surrounding the stage. Some people were vacating it since the performance had finished, several of whom greeted me with high fives.

"Armi! Long time, no see!"

"Uy, kamusta na?"

"Bye Armi!"

"Hoooy, Armi!" Shawi's voice came from behind me.

I felt pounding on my back and looked up to see the rest of my bandmates come off the stage and take their seats around the table.

Frank Lloyd's hand was already raised to order drinks from the waiter passing by. "Pare, caramel beer, pitchel mo na."

"Hi, Ate Armi!" Jen gave me a big smile as she took the seat next to me. "Buti nakaabot ka. Kakarating mo lang?"

"Hoy, 'wag n'yo nga kausapin 'yan." Boboy waved me away even as he swung his leg over the bench seat to sit down across the table. "Nilayasan na tayo n'yan. You're cancelled, man, cancelled."

Jen laughed and I made another face.

"Gaano katagal pa ba 'yang trabaho na 'yan, Armi? Mahigit isang buwan ka na diyan, ano?" Shawi leaned over the table to sneak a grab of someone else's buffalo wings leftovers on the table.

"Hay nako, pwede huwag natin pag-usapan 'yan. Langya 'to," I spoke up in my defense. "Akala n'yo naman binigyan ako ng choice 'no?"

It had been six weeks since I started my new job at Tito Boy's construction company.

The receptionist role was certainly simple but it was the constant exposure to Tito Boy's obnoxious behavior that made the job completely unappealing.

If only he went one day without asking the slightly plump office manager when she was going to go on a diet, or bragging about his son's libido, or constantly talking about why men are better than women.

I was sure I could already guess why their former receptionist had quit. Not to mention the fact that the job was in Cavite, so to avoid the traffic, I always had to leave super early in the morning and return late at night. It barely left me any free time as it was. I wasn't two weeks into the job when I'd already wanted to quit too.

Except, I knew I couldn't.

Shawi reached over and smacked Boboy behind the head. "Ito namang si Boboy. Pati mga set natin, cancel na lang ng cancel. Paano ba tayo uunlad n'yan?"

"Kailangan natin ng bagong gimik," Frank Lloyd proposed, propping his elbows on the table. "Pang-marketing. May kakilala ako doon sa recording studio sa President's Av. May recommended siya na videographer taga-Makati. Baka pwede daw tayong tulungan gumawa ng MTV."

"Madali lang gumawa ng YouTube channel," Jen supplied even with her face tilted down, preoccupied over her mobile phone. "Kung sumikat ang video n'yo, pwedeng big time na 'yan! Grabe kaya ang social media ngayon, in case hindi n'yo alam."

"Nasaan na ba si mahiwagang idol George, Armi?" Shawi asked, licking sauce off his fingers.

"Oo nga," Frank Lloyd agreed. "Sabi niya ipapakilala daw niya tayo kay Ryan, yung friend niya na ka-close ni Kuya Ely."

George had come along to jam with us at my house a few weeks ago and he was his usual entertaining self; impressing Shawi with his freestyle drum technique, charming the hell out of my mom and Jen, and getting the appropriate sympathy after again relaying his unfortunate dealings with Will whom everyone now concluded to be the devil incarnate.

I only managed a shrug. Personally, I was so over the whole George thing. I'd even seen some pictures of his new girlfriend from his phone—*Katya*. I honestly thought I would be more upset or jealous but maybe Ate Roweena's patience and tolerance were finally rubbing off on me.

Just then, a pitcher of beer arrived along with a fresh platter of snacks and my eyes lit up when I recognized the guy carrying it as the owner of the bar. He was a friendly rotund guy who was a few years older than us. He and Frank Lloyd had both gone to the same high school in the area.

"Uy!" I greeted with a big smile. "Kuya Theo, kamusta na po?"

"O, Armi!" he replied gaily as he set down the tray on the table. "Buti naman nakaabot ka ngayong gabi."

"Ayos. Nachos." Shawi rubbed his hands eagerly as he surveyed the food platter, already reaching out to help himself and Frank Lloyd smacked his hand away so he could be first.

I ignored them and shot Theo a questioning look. "Ano ba 'yan, Kuya Theo? Nawala lang ako sandali, nalugi na 'tong bar mo?" I pointed at the big banner behind the stage.

Theo chuckled. "Hay nako, Armi. Mahirap na talaga ang panahon ngayon. Pasensiya na ha," he began. "Wala na kayong lugar na matutugtugan. Maliban na lang kung gusto n'yong bumisita sa main branch namin sa Commonwealth."

"Ang layo naman!" Shawi made a face, pausing mid-drink of his beer. "Wala na ba talagang magagawa?"

Frank Lloyd patted Theo's back. "Kung ano man, malaki ang utang na loob namin sa'yo, pare."

Boboy was already shaking his head. "At siguradong ma-mi-miss ka namin at itong paborito naming tambayan." He lifted his beer mug to toast. "Kuya Theo. Cheers!"

And everyone clinked mugs. "Cheers!"

Theo bid everyone thanks before he waved and headed back to the bar to get back to work.

"Oy, ubos na 'yung fries? Ang bilis mo naman, Shawi!" Jen complained.

"Teka, teka," Boboy started, his tone authoritative. "Balik tayo sa usapan. Siryoso ba kayo sa MTV na 'yan?"

Frank Lloyd shrugged. "Bakit naman hindi? Pwede naman natin subukan, right?"

"Basta ba kumpleto tayo eh." Boboy gave me a pointed look, his displeasure at my having ditched them for the past few weeks absolutely not disguised. "Kailan ka ba pwede, Armi?"

"Sabihan n'yo lang ako. Kung importante naman, maga-gawan ng paraan 'yan eh," I replied, putting my hands up. "Tignan n'yo, umabot naman ako today, diba?"

Jen elbowed me, her eyes lighting up. "Uy, Ate. Today ba 'yung kasal ni Ate Stella? Kaya ka walang pasok?"

"Ah, kasal nga pala ni Stella kanina 'no?" Shawi mumbled through a mouthful of nachos.

I nodded. "Napagamit tuloy ako ng ginintuang VL ng hindi oras. Buti na lang pinayagan ako ng bossing."

"Kamusta na pala sila Ate Weena at si Kuya Lance? Kasama ba sila sa kasal kanina?" Jen wanted to know, her expression eager, already scandalous.

"Hoyst Jennifer, wag ka nga chismosa," Boboy told her off.

Jen shook her head. "Hindi, sinusundan ko 'to eh. Mas maganda pa kaysa sa telenobela."

I pursed my lips, taking a moment to consider my response to her question.

The short answer was that Lance had done the unexpected and ghosted on her. It wouldn't have mattered to me but I felt really sorry for Ate Roweena.

Lance had stopped messaging her altogether. And I had heard in passing that when Ate Roweena had run into Cattleya once last month during her training assignment in Makati, Cattleya didn't seem too happy to see her, let alone want to hang out again.

It was wholly depressing to think about, as it was a stark reminder that even someone like Ate Roweena could be led on and strung along like that. My sister always put on a brave face but I knew better than anyone how absolutely heart-broken she must be. Notwithstanding my mother who hadn't gone one day since without lamenting how Ate Roweena missed out on such a great catch.

"Abangan ang susunod na kabanata," I replied to Jen with a careless shrug, not wanting to burden her with the mundane details.

I, on the other hand, couldn't help but think that at least, given how things had played out, my sister could finally move on and not have to bend over backwards for these superficial people's approval any longer.

Some mornings, on the way to work, I would share a tricycle with one of our neighbors heading to the main road to catch the bus on the highway. We would pass the big compound across the street at 214 *San Antonio Avenue* where the little door in the forbidding gate that I had almost gotten used to being open was shut again as the house returned to its silent state, just like it had been for decades.

In any case, the superficial people did not attend Nick and Stella's wedding today so honestly, they came to my mind even less. Especially since being one of Stella's bridesmaids had kept me even busier throughout the several weeks leading to the big day.

"O ano, bukas, pwede kayo?" Boboy started, his eyebrows raised. "At least tignan natin 'yang videographer sa Makati." He gave everyone a look before his gaze settled on me expectantly.

But I was already making another face.

Stella's wedding had been completely exhausting. She had mandated a bridal shower spa party and a bar-hopping bachelorette party—both of which had been events I'd been tasked to arrange.

Not to mention helping organize the wedding gift registry and practically scavenging every trinket and *pasalubong* shop in the greater Metro Manila area to find the quaint little *bahay kubo* chimes that had been given away as their wedding souvenir.

And after the wedding, when I thought I would finally be off the hook, at the last minute, Stella had made another bridesmaid request that apparently, I wasn't allowed to refuse.

17

Sabit

I stared at the buildings we passed by on the SLEX. I was still a bit groggy from the previous night's gimik but Stella had come by to pick me up earlier than I would have preferred for a Sunday morning. I let out a sigh before turning to her in the car. "Kailangan ba talaga kasama ako sa garden party 'yan?"

Stella made a face even as she kept her eyes on the road while driving. "Armi naman," she chided. "Si Tita ang may pakana ng brunch na 'yan. Alangan naman na tumanggi ako. Ni hindi ko nga kilala yung mga pupunta eh. I think mga fans ni Tita. Iiwan mo ako mag-isa kasama ang mga 'yon?"

I rolled my eyes. Though I knew full well what it was like to be indebted to people enough that you had no choice but to acquiesce to their requests. I figured it must be like the Pinoy mafia. In any case, I had to admit I was also curious to finally be meeting Nick's illustrious "Tita."

"Pinatawag ko pa 'yang last minute na i-add ka sa guest list kaya," Stella added. "Buti na lang madali ma-convince si Nick. Alam mo naman 'yon, kailangan lang i-align lahat sa point of view niya, okay ka na."

I chuckled as I knew exactly what she meant. In which case, Stella had definitely found her perfect match. I flicked her shoulder with a mischievous grin. "So? Anong feeling ng bagong kasal?"

Stella waved me away. "Oo na, oo na. Alam mo naman ako eh, practical lang, simple lang. Never naman ako naghanap ng kakikiligan. At mabait naman 'yan si Nick."

I regarded her expression with a small, possibly impressed, smile. She looked at peace, settled. And despite my personal opinion about Nick, I was happy for my friend.

Although I was sure I would miss having her living in the same barangay. As with tradition, Stella had moved in with Nick into his parents' house in Forbes, and with Nick's parents still in Dubai, she was now the mistress of his mansion.

Before long, Stella turned off the main highway, heading down another road and driving by a security gate where the guard recognized her and waved us through.

I'd never been inside the private subdivision of Forbes Park in Makati before myself. I'd always heard it was the "Beverly Hills of Manila" where mostly expats, diplomats, and wealthy people lived.

I glanced back at the several large houses we were driving past. They were all so beautiful and clean-looking. It almost looked like we were driving on a street in an entirely different country.

Stella turned the wheel to head down another wide avenue

lined with acacia and mahogany trees and clicked the blinker again to turn towards a high black wrought iron gate, between stone walls covered in well-manicured green creeper plants.

I peered out the windshield up at the house, my jaw already dropping even as the gate opened and Stella drove onto a small rotunda driveway fronting the house itself.

For the love of god, there was a working three-tier ceramic fountain in the middle of the driveway. "Oh my shiyeeeet…" I murmured.

Stella noticed the look on my face. "Ah. Yan. Ang katas ng imperyo ng Tita Fely's cooking products."

I was so in awe, I couldn't keep my mouth closed.

The two-story mansion was a classic Spanish-style structure built with cobblestone walls, capiz windows, and what were probably imported tiles that I was almost sure I would hear all about from Nick during the course of the morning. There was a crisp green lawn immediately adjacent to the driveway accessible through a pretty little archway.

When Stella and I got out of the car, I could already see that the garden was set up with a long table, decorated with a pristine white tablecloth, delicate floral plates, fancy cups, gold candles, shiny silver tiered cake stands, and fresh flower centerpieces.

The whole scene was blessed by the fortunate mild weather. It almost looked like a set from a movie. Several servers wearing clean, white uniforms bustled about getting things ready while a handful of other girls about my age dressed in their Sunday's best were milling about, drinking freaking champagne in *not* cheap plastic party cups.

I was suddenly glad I'd let Ate Roweena lend me one of her 'For Special Occasions Only' sundresses to wear. Otherwise, my maong-and-T-shirt combo would have absolutely stuck out like—*me at this brunch.*

"Stella, Armi, you're here!" Nick greeted us with a big grin as he strolled out of the double front doors of the house. He held his hand out to Stella to beckon her over. "Tara na. Tita's waiting." He glanced back at me as if appraising my clothes before mumbling, "I guess pwede na 'yan. Na-mention ko na naman kay Tita na hindi ka taga-Forbes."

I bit my lip in incredulity.

Nick had always been in near competition with my mom for tactlessness. The only difference being Nick's manner was always so self-assured and pretentious, it was often more amusing than insulting.

But then Nick switched his countenance, waving his arm to gesture around us as we walked towards the garden setup. "Isn't this house amazing? Paalala mo sa'kin I have to show you that new painting Tita got from Alex Manlapig. She already had a huge collection of her work. Even before the artist got so famous," he was saying. "Doesn't Tita have such good taste?" Then he turned to Stella. "Pala, Stella," he began. "Can you make a note? Tita said 'yung Philips na air fryer ang bilhin natin. Mas maganda daw ang quality kaysa that other one."

My eyebrows rose in bemusement at the sort of mundane things that Nick's "Tita" felt compelled to concern herself with. But before I could ponder any further about the kind of person she was, the lady of the house herself burst out of the front doors. The mere bustle of her entrance drew everyone's attention.

Tita was taller than I had imagined and she definitely walked with the stately, authoritative air that matched her social status. She wore a colorful, patterned, flowy dress which worked with her pearl necklace and mother-of-pearl earrings.

I could tell she dyed her hair, probably to hide the gray, but because of that, I couldn't make a guess regarding her age. And even though I could imagine she must be older than my own parents, she seemed to move with an energy, a vibrance, that gave no hint of being elderly.

Tita didn't have servants on either side fanning her with *pamaypays* but she may as well have. The three maids wearing matching uniforms seemed to struggle to keep up with Tita's strides as she sauntered across the garden, making staunch assertions with her clear, decisive voice.

"Nilabhan naman 'yung mga tela na *servilleta* bago hinanda 'no? Sinabi ko na 'yan, maski hindi pa nagamit, hindi natin gustong mag-amoy cabinet 'yon."

"*Opo, ma'am.*"

"At 'yung *cubiertos* na pang-dessert mamaya, pakisabi kay Mylene, ilabas 'yung padala ni Sergio galing States. 'Yun 'yung ka-match nung Corelle na plato."

"*Opo, ma'am.*"

"Ay Elsie, paki-check din muna 'yung mga cheese na binili sa grocery kung malapit na mag-expire. Baka hindi nanaman pinili ni Letty 'yung matagal ang best before date."

"*Opo, ma'am.*"

By that point, Tita had walked up to our little group just past the garden archway. Her sharp eyes turned towards the unfamiliar person first—me, before she looked over at Stella and Nick and broke a regal smile. "Ah, nandito na kayo."

"Hi Tita," Nick beamed his greeting as he leaned in to do the traditional "air kiss" *beso beso* with Tita before gesturing for Stella to do the same.

I didn't presume I was allowed to greet her in such a familiar way so I stayed a step behind Stella.

"O, Stella, iha," Tita began, her eager, open expression still hinting at superiority. "How did you find that Bosch washing machine I recommended? Hindi ba, I was right? It's better than the generic brand. It's rated higher for better water consumption."

Stella's eyes lit up and she nodded. "Ay opo, Tita. Thank you po." She glanced back at me, I supposed intending to do the introductions but Tita spoke first.

"Siya ba yung last minute addition sa guest list?" Tita's eyebrow was raised as she looked me up and down.

"Armi Benitez po." I made a polite nod. "Thank you po for having me, Mrs. San Mateo."

Tita gave me a slight scrutinizing once-over before she called out, "Graciella, iha, *ven aqui!*" She beckoned from behind me.

I was surprised to notice a girl standing quite close to us. I had barely noticed that she was there. Granted, she was wearing a red dress, a stark contrast of color amidst the green garden party, but her presence was so unnoticeable, it almost seemed like she blended into the environment.

"This is my daughter, Graciella," Tita gestured to her.

Graciella merely tilted her head in acknowledgment. Nothing about her stood out at all. In fact, I would have noticed the *yaya* hovering around her, holding the little blue medical bag, first.

But I gave them both a smile. "Hi, nice to meet you po."

Graciella didn't reply, barely even looked up again. I almost had to wonder if it wasn't a higher level of snobbery at work. But it was more likely that she was the silent, withdrawn type, possibly a trait resulting from having a super dominating mother.

Nick turned to me to mumble, "Diba, I told you? Isn't Graciella super classy?"

Just then, an eruption of hushed squeals caught my attention and I turned to look in time to see a familiar face walk through the doorway.

I blinked in astonishment. "Will."

Will was wearing his usual collared work shirt under a dark suit jacket as he strode out to the garden, followed by another slightly older guy I didn't recognize.

Meanwhile, half a dozen of Tita's groupies standing around by the table were peering at Will, excitedly whispering to each other as though a movie star had just arrived.

Will gave me a steady look. "Armi."

Tita cast me a glance. "You know my *inaanak*?"

I met Tita's curious gaze again and gave her a short nod to relay, "Uh, yes po. Kapitbahay po namin sina Lance Ortega at their new house sa south."

Nick's face looked like he'd just seen an apparition. "Will!

Pare, I didn't know you would be at this party," he breathed with a reverent tone as he came up, holding out his hand to shake Will's.

Will simply shot him a strange look but his response was directed to the entire group. "I had to drop off some paperwork," he replied nonchalantly. "Tita mentioned she was hosting a brunch and asked us to stay."

The guy standing two steps behind Will came up and put his hand out to shake mine. "Joseph Rivera, pinsan ako ni Will," he volunteered with a friendly smile.

I noted his mismatched beige blazer and limited edition Nike's and shook his hand, returning his smile. "Hi. Armi. Nice to meet you."

I don't know why but Joseph's eyes lit up at the confirmation of my name. "Armi?" he repeated, almost looking astonished. "Well then, it's nice to finally meet you."

18

Sa Apoy

When the bell rang for brunch (like there was literally a bell), there was some shuffling around the table as Nick wanted to sit next to Will and Tita, Stella wanted to sit next to Nick and me, Joseph wanted to sit across from me, and Tita's groupies wanted to sit anywhere with a clear view of Will. Meanwhile, I wanted to sit next to Stella and as far away as I could from Tita and Nick.

I ended up seated between Will and Stella, across from Joseph and Nick, while Tita and Graciella sat at each end of the long table, with the rest of Tita's groupies occupying the rest of the seats.

It wasn't the most ideal seating arrangement in my opinion. But it was hard to think about anything else once the servers came out with the food.

My eyes widened in delight as several trays and plates of cupcakes, sandwiches, and French pastries were laid out on the table. I was seriously tempted to stuff some in my bag to take home. I was regretting not having my mother's giant Louis Vuitton knockoff luggage bag with me. But of course, I was pretty sure it would be absolutely frowned upon...right? Right?

I looked around again in appreciation of the ambiance.

The atmosphere around the table was fortunately informal. The random girls were chattering to themselves, sneaking glances at Will. Stella was already helping herself to the food. Tita was turned to one side giving more instructions to the servers standing by—something about making sure the kitchen had enough supply of tube ice for everyone's drinks.

One of the server guys was coming around to ask whether we wanted to have tea or coffee. He came to Will first.

"Coffee." Will gave him a short nod.

I gave the guy a small smile. "Ako rin, please."

The guy left and I was marveling at the fancy sugar cubes melting in my coffee when Will cleared his throat and turned to me.

"How's..."

I looked up at him warily since he seemed to be on the verge of the dreaded "small talk" and I couldn't imagine what conversation he imagined we were going to have.

He paused before concluding, "the dog?"

My eyes lit up in bemusement. "Ah, si Basti?" I supplied. "Okay naman."

Just then, I realized the unique opportunity I had been given. To fish for information. Since Will, being Lance's supposed best friend, might be able to provide some insight with regards to Lance's motivations for ditching my sister. Not that I could ask him directly about it.

"Si…Ate Roweena pala naka-assign sa Makati this month," I began tentatively. "I think sa BTI Tower mismo 'yung training nila. Baka nakikita niyo siya around nila Lance."

But Will shook his head, his focus returning to his plate. "No, not really."

"Anong nga ba'ng course mo sa college, iha?"

The sudden loud question made me jump a little bit in a startle.

Tita hadn't called me by name but it seemed obvious to everyone that her question was directed at me.

I met her gaze to reply politely, "Socio po."

Tita formed a serene smile and gave me a nod. "Ah, you're pre-law."

"Ay, hindi po."

She tilted her head. "Pre-med?"

"Hindi po."

Her perfectly-shaped eyebrows rose up. "You must be taking over the family business then. What does your father do?"

"May commission po ng taxi si Dad."

Her mouth formed an 'o' as if in sympathy, or condescension, whatever. "Are any of your siblings going into law or medicine? Even nursing?"

I shook my head. "Um, wala po."

Tita rapped her fingers on the table in deep thought like she was deeply disturbed, as though she had been exclusively tasked to solve my entire life. "What about—nauuso ngayon ang entrepreneurship." She glanced at the rest of the group to call attention to her statement. "I recently encouraged someone from the country club to start a passion project— her own homemade craft-making business. It's gotten quite successful," she declared with a proud smile as though she was fully instrumental to the fact before going on. "Maski she has a day job as a real estate agent. She was really grateful for my recommendation." Then she turned to me to prompt, "Mayroon ka ba'ng extracurricular clubs or hobbies?"

"Ay, opo." I nodded. "I'm part of a local indie-alternative band."

I swear to god, time must have frozen.

Tita was staring at me with her mouth open. It was a few seconds before she asked, "You're...in a band?"

Out of the corner of my eye, I noticed Nick making a face as if he was talking to himself in agreement with Tita and I didn't have to guess that he was mocking me in his head. I was aware he'd never had a good opinion about my band either.

Joseph only looked highly entertained by the conversation. I couldn't see Stella's reaction from behind me or that she was in fact, trying to interject something in my defense, but I could see Will continuing to eat his food, seeming completely unperturbed by what was going on.

"Yes po," I replied if only to fill the void of silence. "Mga kaibigan ko po from college. We play small gigs in local bars sa south. Although our regular venue actually closed down so we'll be looking at other options."

When Tita spoke again, her tone was almost incredulous. "So you have no sustainable career path and you're not yet married. Aren't you worried about your future?"

I looked around the table only slightly wary at everyone

staring at me and only just then saw Stella's supportive, slightly embarrassed smile. But honestly, I'd been through years of judgment about my band from my own mother enough that I was unfazed by their reactions.

I managed a resigned smile and made sure my tone was not defensive. "I think hindi naman po conclusive na because I'm in a band, delikado po ang future ko. At saka marami nama'ng successful people who are still single, diba po?"

Tita's jaw dropped, her eyes widening at my response—or more to the point, my audacity *to* respond.

I met Nick's equally stunned, almost horrified gaze. I guessed nobody was used to Tita's opinions being contradicted, much less Tita herself. I cracked a smirk and tried to lighten the mood. "Diba si Taylor Swift nga po, wala pa ri'ng asawa?"

All I heard was Stella snorting back her chuckle.

Stella grabbed my arm as we left the table once the meal was finished and everything was being put away. "Nag-'thank you' na ba ako sa'yo?" She turned an imploring face up at me and batted her eyelashes, knowing full well she owed me one, most especially after that meal.

I gave her a warning look. "Oh my god, ang utang mo sa'kin. I feel like nag-job interview ako bigla."

I glanced back to see Will and Joseph having a conversation with Tita across the garden while Nick was enjoying the attention of a few of Tita's groupies. "Pwede na ba akong umuwi?" I wanted to know.

Stella shook her head. "Hindi pa." She led my arm back

to the house, through the sliding doors, to the large room just beyond. It was a living room with high ceilings, brocade curtains, and a polished wooden floor.

My eyes lit up as I spotted the beautiful *Fazioli* piano in the corner. It was shiny and black and covered with an intricate lace throw. "Wow, ang ganda ng piano! Ano ba 'yan, may program mamaya? Talent show?" I mocked in ridicule, although I had to admit I wasn't too nervous in that case, since I was pretty good at playing the piano.

Stella laughed with an almost mischievous, sardonic manner. "I wish."

She tugged me past the living room, through another doorway, into another large room where about ten counter-top tables had been arranged in rows.

Each table was fitted with an electric plate, a stack of silver pots, glass mixing bowls, wooden spoons, and other equipment. Some of the girls from the brunch were already at their "stations" getting ready.

My eyes widened almost instantly in dread.

"Tita is giving everyone a cooking class."

I could have sworn I paled white as rice.

Cooking was absolutely *not* my forte. I mean I knew how to boil an egg. But in college, I subsisted almost entirely on instant cup noodles—just like everyone else.

Needless to say, in my family, aside from my mom, it was Ate Roweena who wore the ruffled apron.

I didn't have to glare at Stella. I knew she could already feel it. "Ang utang mo, Stella. Dumadami ha."

19

Class

I squinted at the laminated recipe card on my table. It was a recipe for making *Adobong manok sa gata* of which half of the ingredients were trademarked *Tita Fely's* products.

I glanced up to meet Stella's gaze as she looked back at me. Tita had assigned her the very front table while I was at the one just behind her.

Apparently, among her many celebrated occupations, Tita also offered Home Economics classes out of her house and the girls invited to the brunch, most of whom were engaged or already married, were actually all from her class.

I gathered that Tita was getting Stella into the fold probably to ensure that she was going to be a good wife and homemaker.

I could tell from the look on Stella's face that this was her true motive for insisting that I come along today and while I didn't like it, I completely understood why she didn't let me know in advance.

Stella definitely knew that bringing me along would work to her advantage since Tita's attention had to be split between the two newcomers—us, instead of being solely focused on her.

Though as the lesson went on, I had to admit it was more constructive than I'd thought it would be. The general discussions ranged to topics beyond cooking and food. The whole class was actually more about self-reliance, not being dependent on your spouse, having your own goals, and being in charge of your life.

It was pretty impressive.

Then again, Tita really was an impressive person.

That was, you know, if you managed to get past her overwhelming meddlesome and condescending nature first.

For most of the class, I'd forgotten about Nick, Will, and Joseph and had no idea what they had got up to. Then amidst the instruction to simmer the *adobo* sauce, Will and Joseph came through the doorway.

I had a feeling they were intending to cross the room and go elsewhere, possibly to do some work. Will's phone was in his hand as though he was about to make a call or had just gotten off of one. But when Tita looked up to acknowledge the two guys' presence with a smile, they both stopped walking.

"Ay, iho, kamusta pala si Monica?" Tita directed a question at Will. "Did she like my new cookbook?"

Will turned to her and nodded. "Opo, Ninang. She's almost perfected your *paella* recipe," he relayed. "She also took a course from a Michelin-star chef a few months ago. She loved it."

"Maganda 'yan," Tita affirmed. "If she works hard, she can achieve excellence. If you practice excellence every day, you will be excellent by nature." Then her volume rose as she addressed the whole class. "That's something to keep in mind, girls. Practice makes permanent."

There were murmurings of *Yes, Tita's* around the whole group and I looked around, my mouth slightly hanging open, marveling at everyone's complete faith in Tita's words of wisdom.

Will glanced over at me for a second before he stepped back to one side of the room, bending his head to check his phone, looking busy.

My gaze moved from him to meet Joseph's, who gave me a bright smile as he walked over to my station. "Gusto mo ba ng tulong?" he offered.

I sneaked a peek up at Tita, who was preoccupied speaking to one of the maids about replacing all the spent toilet paper rolls with full new ones in all the guest bathrooms in the house or something before I looked back at him with my hushed reply. "Baka pagalitan ka ni Tita. Patapos na'ko anyway." I peered into my *kaldero* to stir the sauce a few times.

Unlike all the other girls, I had managed to make an absolute mess of my cooking. Soy sauce was splattered across the countertop and my apron. There were peppercorns everywhere, including on the floor. And my sauce had previously boiled over so there was a pool of coconut milk sizzling around my hot plate.

I craned my neck to check Stella's countertop. Hers

remained neat and tidy and she was wholly concentrated on simmering her sauce. *Whatever.* She was going to make Nick a great wife. I resisted the urge to roll my eyes.

Joseph cast my work area an amused look and I wrinkled my nose at his obvious appraisal.

"Bakit nga pala yung mga guys hindi kasali dito sa cooking class?"

He chuckled. "Tita likes very traditional gender roles," he explained. "As a family matriarch, siya lagi ang in charge sa lahat ng bagay, especially sa bahay."

"And she certainly seems to have an opinion on everything," I quipped, unable to help it.

Joseph nodded in full agreement, his eyes twinkling. "She's pretty hands-on. You could say it's also why she's so successful." He watched me blowing on a spoon to taste the sauce and held out his hand for it so he could try it too.

"Mm," he mumbled in approval. "Masarap ha."

"Ayos." I grinned, giving him a high-five. My gaze was distracted when I spotted Will, who had finished up with his phone, walking over to us. He had that usual look on his face that seemed intended to intimidate people.

But I met his gaze, my eyebrow slightly raised in defiance and once he was within earshot, I turned slightly to Joseph to remark, "Tignan mo 'yang pinsan mo. Maninindak pa. Buti na lang astig ako. Maski Michelin-star chef pa yung kapatid niya."

Will's expression didn't change when he replied, "I think alam naman natin lahat na magugunaw muna ang buong mundo bago pa ipanganak yung kung sino ma'ng actually makaka-sindak sa'yo."

That comment made me laugh as, despite Will's blank expression, it sounded like he fully believed what he'd just said, like he knew he wasn't making a joke at all.

"Talaga 'to si Will," Joseph chided. "'Wag mo naman sirain ang first impressions ni Armi sa'tin."

I laughed again. "Nako, Joseph. Medyo late na for that."

Joseph shot Will a strange look. "Ah, talaga? May sala na kaagad sa'yo si Will? I can't believe it."

"Believe it." I nodded before tilting my head in the recall. "Nako, noong first time ko siya na-meet sa barangay fiesta namin, ang lakas niya mang-lait. Sabi ba naman niya hindi daw magaling tumugtog yung banda—"

"Ah, eh, baka naman—"

"Namin," I finished, giving Joseph a pointed look and he almost choked in surprise.

Will was staring at me with a sort of glare but he didn't say anything to defend himself.

I smirked and went on. "Maski sino siguro tanungin mo sa barangay, iisa lang ang sasabihin tungkol kay Will." I paused for effect and whispered, "*Suplado.*"

Joseph burst out laughing so suddenly, he spilled what remained of the spoonful of sauce he was still holding onto his beige shirt and he yelped out loud. "Ah! Hala, nako— teka lang." He immediately whirled around to head for the bathroom.

Will's forehead creased as he watched Joseph retreat to clean himself up before he shifted his gaze back to meet mine. "You must have heard me say that out of context," he pointed out.

I raised my eyebrows in incredulity, suppressing the urge to chuckle. "Anong context?"

He pursed his lips. "Na gusto ko na'ng umalis kasi hindi ako komportable." He tilted his head, his voice low as if it displeased him to admit a weakness. "Hindi lang talaga ako magaling makihalo sa mga taong hindi ko kilala."

"Eh, kung hindi ka naman mag-make ng effort para kilalanin ang mga tao, if you don't keep doing it, talagang walang mangyayari sa'yo. Sabi nga ni Tita diba, everyday practice makes excellence," I relayed with a comical shrug.

Will seemed to consider my statement but he didn't say anything. He simply reached over to dip his finger across the cooking spoon on the table to taste the sauce.

20

Utang na loob

After the class, the staff began to clear everything away. Nick had finally come back and Tita pulled him and Stella aside, possibly to share some more nuggets of wisdom for newlyweds. I didn't want to intrude in their private conversation so I stepped back out to the garden first.

Everyone else must have been inside since the garden was empty. The long brunch table had been folded and put away so I was only just noticing the colors of the garden itself. Every bush surrounding the green Bermuda lawn had a different kind of blooming flower. There were three distinct colors of bougainvillea, pink and yellow gumamelas, yellow bells, and an assortment of blue flowers whose names I didn't know. I could smell sampaguita from somewhere but I couldn't see where it was.

"Armi."

I glanced back and smiled at Joseph, coming out of the sliding doors towards me. "O, nalinis mo na yung damit mo?"

He gave me a sheepish grin. "Pasalamat na lang na gata 'yung sauce. Hindi toyo."

I had to laugh, looking back out the garden, and folded my arms across my chest.

"Ang ganda 'no?" Joseph prompted. He pointed to the far corner where there was a Virgin Mary grotto and began to walk towards it. "I remember Tita wanted to pave all this and extend the parking lot. Buti na lang hindi niya ginawa."

I followed behind him. "Yung house nila Nick sa kabila, Stella said they don't have a big garden, pero may swimming pool." I peered up at the trees where wind chimes were hanging and tinkling in the light breeze and after a moment, I smiled. "But I think oo nga, mas maganda ganito."

"I'm sure madalas silang ma-iinvite dito anyway. Tita seems to like Stella and Nick a lot."

"Oh, yes." I nodded in full agreement. "I guess sakto talaga dito si Nick. Wala siyang kapares tumugon ng utang na loob. And he really enjoys having Tita to look up to."

"Only child lang si Graciella," Joseph rationalized. "So I think Tita's taken it upon herself na asikasuhin din ang mga inaanak at pamangkin niya. Will especially is her favorite among all of us," he remarked with a catch in his tone. "And ngayon na kapitbahay na nila sila Nick, she has another *ampon* to take care of."

Take care of or meddle with? I wanted to comment but didn't.

Either way, I was one-hundred percent sure that Tita's interference was one-hundred percent welcome in Nick's case.

I gestured back to the house. "So, uwian na ba?" I asked, hoping my eagerness to leave wouldn't be so obvious.

But Joseph shook his head with a grin. "Tita loves entertaining. They're just setting up for *merienda cena* inside now."

My eyes popped wide open. "Hindi nga!" I made a face. Was I going to be stuck in this house with these people all day?

I craned my neck to check where Stella was again but right then, I couldn't see her. She must have gone into another room with Tita and the girls. "Dito na din ba kayo mag-di-dinner?" I wanted to know, almost half in dread.

He shrugged good-naturedly. "Siguro. Tita will probably insist anyway. As you may have noticed, she doesn't like to be refused." He added, "Although depende din kay Will. Dakilang alalay lang ako today."

I blinked and scoffed in mocking. "Wow, taking advantage," I jeered. "Sana naman hindi ka lang laging nagpapa-uto diyan sa pinsan mo ha."

Joseph was already shaking his head. "Hindi naman sa ganoon. Ganti lang din naman sa tulong niya sa'kin. Grabe maasikaso 'yan si Will. Hindi mo ba napansin?"

I pursed my lips, entirely not convinced of this altruism. "Well, I guess he certainly has the means." I supposed it should be pretty easy to help people if you were in the same financial situation as Mr. Will Salcedo AKA *Mayaman pa sa Diyos*.

"And more," Joseph added with no hint of doubt in his tone. "Ang swerte ng girlfriend n'yan kung sakali."

I couldn't help another chuckle as I could barely imagine Will's ego making space for another person. I leaned closer to the bushes to smell the fragrant jasmine flowers.

"He's very supportive. Maski sa mga kaibigan n'ya," he relayed with a tinge of commendation in his tone. "Kapag may problema, kahit ano pa 'yan, talagang gagawin niya ang lahat para makatulong." His voice hushed as he went on. "Ang pagkarinig ko nga recently, tinulungan n'ya yung best friend niya'ng si Lance makatakas sa babae."

My ears instantly perked up.

Will helped Lance do what?

I thought I almost stopped breathing altogether. I cleared my throat, straightening up, trying to look disinterested, but my stomach was already queasy, almost instinctively knowing where this conversation was going to go.

But Joseph didn't offer any more information so I had to prompt, "Ah...ano daw nangyari?"

Honestly, I was still hedging on the chance that perhaps Lance had picked up some other girl that Will had saved him from, meaning, *after* my sister. But what were the odds of that? It had to be one huge, giant coincidence. It just had to be.

Joseph shrugged. "Pinagpayuhan daw niya yung friend niya about this girl na dapat layuan."

I curled my lips in distaste, turning my head to make sure Joseph couldn't see. "Kasi mahirap lang sila, right?"

"Um, no yata." He shook his head. "I think pangit na family daw." His voice hushed even lower as if to indicate a big scandal. "Nakakahiya. I mean, of course, hindi 'yan pwede para sa pamilyang Ortega. Mabuti na lang nakita ni Will."

I clenched my teeth, my heart pounding loud in my ears. There was no other person to whom Joseph could have been referring. There was absolutely no doubt about it. He was talking about my Ate Roweena and my socially inept, socially unsuitable, poor, poor family.

And Will.

Will was the person who had ordered Lance to stay away.

That arrogant, self-important, condescending jerk had used his manipulative powers over the gullible, weak-minded, naïve Lance.

And convinced him to break my sister's faultless heart.

I was hurriedly fixing my bag (the *macarons* wrapped in tissue I had stuffed in it were making it a pain to zip closed and Jen was going to have to be happy with squashed ones) when Will appeared at the foyer, saw the despondent look on my face, and the fact that I was about to leave.

"Anong nangyari?" Will almost looked concerned.

I tried to wave it *and him* away. "Um, may kailangan nga pala akong i-meet na friends sa Greenbelt."

His eyebrows rose in question. "Nagpaalam ka na kay Ninang?"

I nodded. In fact, I had noted that my early exit seemed all too welcome to Tita's groupies. Not that I could blame them. This house was definitely not my scene and I figured Stella should be able to manage from this point on. I'd already fought her fight. I was so done. Bridesmaid's duties fulfilled. "Hindi makaalis si Stella because it's her party, so—" I gestured to Joseph because he had volunteered to drop me off.

Will nodded and cut in, "Hatid na kita." He reached over to grab the keys from Joseph's hand before looking up to meet his gaze. "Ako na, Joseph. Pasok ka na sa loob," he bid his cousin.

I'd already looked up to meet Joseph's gaze with a grimace,

intending to protest since Will was the person I was trying to get away *from*. But Joseph simply pursed his lips and disappeared back through the door into the house.

I retched in my head in disbelief and displeasure. *Ampf—*

21

So Yabang

It may have just been a fifteen-minute ride but the silence in the car was deafening. At least to me. And it was definitely uncomfortable silence.

I clenched my fists, my entire body tense.

And Will was so self-involved, he didn't even notice I was practically radiating with hate in the passenger seat.

Then again, even Joseph had claimed, Will had thought he had done a good deed. He probably thought he was completely blameless in the matter. He probably had enough confidence to think he had the authority to stick his nose into other people's businesses.

I almost cursed everything in creation for the simple fact that we had to cross EDSA to get to my destination and I hoped against hope that for once, just for today, people would be civilized and not clog up the road with annoying traffic.

But soon enough, the buildings of Ayala Center weaved into view and I blew out a breath in relief.

Will drove up the Greenbelt 5 driveway and then hopped out of the car himself.

I was sure it wasn't to feign gentlemanliness and open my door for me because since I couldn't wait to get away from him, I had already opened the door without even waiting for the car to come full stop and jumped out as soon as I could.

But Will walked up to a uniformed guy by a kiosk and I realized he was having his car valet parked.

Of course, it meant I had to wait for him to step away from the kiosk to thank him for the ride—you know, because I have manners.

But after I'd said "thank you" to him and walked away heading towards Greenbelt 3, Will fell into step beside me.

After a few steps, I glanced up at him sideways in abject puzzlement. "May pupuntahan ka?"

He met my gaze, his expression sort of caught off-guard, but he didn't reply right away. He seemed to hesitate about something and we walked a good few more feet before he turned to me.

His gaze was somewhere else as he began to continually shake his head, muttering, "I can't, I can't not say it. I just have to—I have to say it."

I gave him a narrow-eyed, incredibly mystified look. "Anong pinagsasabi mo?"

"Gusto kita."

I stopped short, completely taken aback I had to blink hard. "Eh?" I uttered, almost unintelligibly.

He pursed his lips, looking away as though he was irritated

about the fact itself. "I can't even believe I'm doing this," he began and spoke as though he was doing a monologue, almost as though he was speaking to himself, like I wasn't even there.

"Given the differences in our social stature and financial situation, parang nakakinsulto lang. At siguradong iisipin ng mga kaibigan ko nababaliw na'ko. Hindi ko maubos maisip na magtataka lang ang lahat ng tao for sure. Not to mention labas na labas sa expectations ng pamilya ko ang makibagay sa katulad mo."

He paused and visibly swallowed hard before he actually met my gaze, his tone shifting. "But I hadn't seen you in months. I came to Stella's party kasi gusto kita makita. I couldn't stop thinking about you."

He looked away again, looking frustrated. "Sobrang wala siyang sense. So sige na nga! Hahayaan ko na muna lahat ng katwiran. I need this to be resolved."

I honestly couldn't tell if he was trying to insult me or flatter me, though the self-assured expression on his face was a clear indication that he thought I should be feeling pretty lucky to even be the recipient of his weird speech.

I blinked up at him in total confusion. "Ano...?"

He blew out a seemingly labored breath before he spoke again. "I really...really like you," he said, his gaze pinned on me. Then he cleared his throat, narrowing his gaze before he asked, "Would you please go out with me?"

My jaw was still like on the floor as I stared at him in disbelief. Then after a momentary pause of shock, I snapped to attention, my forehead creasing in distaste and almost mocking before I found my voice. "No," I said with a tone of almost ridicule.

Will winced. He wasn't expecting that. "No," he echoed.

I nodded in confirmation. "No," I repeated.

Will visibly swallowed again. "Okay..." he started, looking at me evenly. "That's...all you have to say?"

I huffed, almost in amusement. "Yeah, ano pa bang extra information ang hinahanap mo?"

He cocked his head to one side, getting annoyed all over again. "Pwede ba'ng isipin mo muna ang sagot mo? After everything *I've* just said, magsusungit ka?"

I shot him a pointed look, my blood seriously starting to boil in hot molten anger. "*Seriously?*" I asked. "After prefacing your speech with how actually insulto ako sa'yo and how iisipin ng mga tao nabaliw ka na, hindi ako pwede magsungit? Sure, sorry, dapat pala matuwa ako!" I threw up my hands.

He shook his head. "Hindi 'yun ang ibig kong sabihin—"

I scoffed, cutting in. "Besides, matapos lahat ng ginawa mo, how could you possibly expect a different answer from me? I *know*, Will," I told him, matter-of-factly. "I know ikaw ang dahilan kung bakit biglang inisnab ni Lance si Ate Weena. I know sumusunod lang siya sa utos mo," I said and Will straightened up as if in recognition, but not denial. I huffed again, shaking my head. "You're not even going to deny it, are you?"

Will pursed his lips again before he gave me another even look. "No."

I looked at him in aghast and scorn. "Bakit mo ginawa 'yun?"

"I was just doing it for his own good," Will explained, his tone all-knowing, authoritative, superior. "It looked like hindi naman masyadong gusto ni Weena si Lance eh. I watched them before. She didn't treat him differently than her other guy friends. Whenever they were together, it didn't look like she returned Lance's feelings."

I rolled my eyes, highly annoyed. "That's just because mahiyain si Ate."

"Maski si Lance thought she wasn't that into him," he told me.

"Kasi ikaw ang nagsabi, siyempre maniniwala si Lance sa'yo!" I burst out, starting to shake my head. "You don't even realize what you've done. You're playing with people's emotions. Just admit it, you thought pera lang ang nakita ni Ate kay Lance."

"Of course not! I never thought that," he said defensively. "Then again, you can't blame someone for thinking it, given your family background."

My eyes widened and I watched him warily. "What *about* my family?"

He sighed, looking away. "Obviously, magkaiba talaga ang situation ng family mo compared kina Lance. If you consider only that pa lang, hindi talaga bagay si Lance at si Weena. But more to the point, Lance's family will expect him to be with someone appropriate, 'yung pati pamilya hindi kailangan alalahanin na baka biglang may gawing nakakahiya, especially in public."

I was stunned again. It was like a physical blow to the face. I knew my family wasn't the freaking Royal Family in terms of social etiquette, but it was quite another thing to hear them being referred to as a public embarrassment.

"Sorry..." Though, I figured it wasn't because he didn't believe what he said. He was sorry for his having to be the one to mention it to me.

I blew out a breath, almost shaking in anger.

Just because he was a rich guy in a position of power, he felt authorized to control other people's decisions, take away their hopes, and manipulate outcomes all merely based on his highly subjective and incredibly *wrong* opinions?

I knew Will was arrogant but I couldn't believe he thought he had the right to decide what was best for other people's lives. Who the hell did he think he was?

But the fact of the matter was that I even already knew it wasn't the first time he had used his influence and done something selfish like this.

After a pause, I looked up at him again. "Pa'no naman si George?"

Will blinked in surprise. "Si George Tañada?" Then he gave me a weird suspicious look. "At ano naman ang concern mo kay George? Best friends na kayo?"

I folded my arms. "Kinwento n'ya sakin yung ginawa mo sa kanya," I started and Will rolled his eyes. "Nahihirapan na nga yung tao—which is kasalanan mo—tapos ikaw pa ang parang galit, ikaw pa ang nagmamataas." I smirked in disdain. "But I suppose dahil ikaw ang may-ari ng kumpanya n'yo, bale wala na lang kung ano man ang mangyari sa iba, right?"

He shook his head again. "Ganyan ang tingin mo sa'kin?" It was more of a statement than a question. "Nainsulto ka lang ng konti, kasalanan ko na ang lahat?"

His expression changed to sneering disbelief when he met my gaze again. "Hindi ako magpapanggap na hindi malayo ng kalagayan natin sa buhay. I have the presence of mind to think of consequences and I don't get distracted by petty things. You don't even know anything about business. You can barely keep a decent job. I, on the other hand, have responsibilities you can't even fathom."

I had to chuckle under my breath. "Oh my god...you are *sooo* yabang!" I exclaimed. "I knew it! I knew it already." I threw up my hands again. "Maski nung unang time kita na-meet, I knew there was seriously *absolutely* no way I was ever going to like you. *Ever*," I concluded firmly as I glared at him.

Will's intense gaze hadn't left mine but his forehead was creased slightly as he studied my face. There was more than anger in his expression, more than offense or frustration. It was as though there was a sudden clarity in his eyes, a finality of understanding brought about by my words. And somehow, a gloomy resignation.

I couldn't stop staring up at him, almost starting to get confused again.

But then he just took a deep breath. "Fine. Sorry," he mumbled before he turned on his heel and left.

My frown deepened and I tried to even out my breathing as I watched him walk away, down the corridor, and past the shops, before disappearing around the corner.

22

Baliktaran

I got your number from Stella.
Don't worry. This text is about business. Not feelings.
I would really appreciate it if you could drop by the office some-time this week.
There's something you need to see.
- W.

I was a bit nervous about the complete punctuation and correct spelling and grammar in Will's text message. It denoted a type of sincere urgency, and so despite my pure hatred for him, I felt compelled to go.

I wanted to catch up with Ate Roweena anyway. Since we were all so busy with work, I hadn't seen my sister in ages. She was just finishing up her weeks of training and her office building just so happened to be conveniently right across from the address that Will had provided.

So when I had a half-day off from work on Thursday be-cause Tito Boy was having the company building fumigated, I took a colorum van all the way to Makati for a *merienda* sister date.

But first, I had to make one stop.

The HMS Group Holdings office in Makati was located in Ayala Triangle's Ayala Tower One, one of the tallest sky-scrapers in the country. It was essentially a big, glass building that towered over everything beneath it. I'd never had a reason to be inside such a building. I almost felt like I was about to go to a job interview again.

My paranoia was kicking in since I felt like the building security was staring at me for wearing rubber shoes and not business casual clothes like the rest of the people purposefully bustling around the lobby.

I probably looked suspiciously out of place but as soon as I told reception where I was headed, they simply pointed me towards the elevators.

It was lunchtime so there were quite a few people coming in and out of the offices all the way up the tower.

When the elevator dinged at the 32nd floor, I peeked out of the doors cautiously. The office smelled of air conditioning, Glade, and coffee.

Across the floor, behind a tall counter with the light-up HMS Holdings Group sign, was a desk on each end, and two people wearing headsets were sitting with their backs to each other.

I glanced to one side out the big floor-to-ceiling windows at the super awesome view. It was a sunny day and I could see the blue skies and puffy clouds all the way clear through to Manila Bay.

I blew out a breath in marvel before I walked up to the counter. I peered at the two executive assistants, waiting for at least one of them to finish up with the phone call they were currently engaged on.

As soon as the girl looked up at me, I cleared my throat quietly. "Um, excuse me. Andyan po ba si...Sir Will?"

"Your name?"

"Uh...Armi. Armi Benitez." I checked her nametag.

Jill.

"Umm..." Jill hummed as she consulted her fancy Samsung Note phone, tapping her stylus loudly. "He—has a board meeting sa Ortigas. He won't be back today anymore." She swiveled her chair around to ask the other guy at the desk behind her. "Uy Jack, may binilin ba si Sir Will sa'yo para kay Ma'am?"

I blinked. Jack. And Jill.

But the other guy who was wearing a vest was nodding as he finished whatever phone call he was on. "That's right. We'll pencil it in. Thank you very much, Mr. Taylor," he bid into his earpiece before he took it off with a flourish, glancing over at Jill. "Benitez ba kamo?"

"Oo."

Jack turned back to his desk and rifled through some folders in a drawer before pulling something out. "Ay, ito. Sir Will left this for you pala, Ma'am," he said, handing something over to me.

I glanced at the manila envelope before looking back at each of them in turn. "Ano 'to?"

Jack rolled his chair backwards so he could elbow Jill and she nodded in understanding. "Pinahanap sa'min ni Sir Will yung past employment records ni Mr. George," he relayed, a sly look on his face.

"His memos, his progress reports—," Jill began to list.

"Hindi niya sinabi kung bakit, pero he said you needed to see them," Jack interjected.

"His KPIs, his performance evaluations," Jill went on.

"He was a terrible employee," Jack supplied, making a face.

"His proposals, his credit statements," Jill kept going.

Jack held his hand around his mouth to whisper loudly, "I heard he was stealing from the company."

And my jaw dropped. "Ano?"

"Huy, hindi ba muntik na siyang ma-promote?" Jack turned to ask Jill, a scandal in his eyes.

Jill nodded again, her expression grave before she explained. "And it's a good thing it didn't happen. It would have meant he had unrestricted access to the financials. Can you imagine?" she asked, looking shocked.

"Buti nakutuban ni Sir Will," Jack continued, giving me a pointed look. "Ang galing talaga ng poging 'yon."

I was rendered incredibly speechless. All I could do was stare at them, the envelope still unopened in my hands.

"Hey, didn't he go out with Miss Monica last year?" Jill began, her eyebrow quirking curiously. "She was so obsessed with him at some point, remember? I always had to book really expensive restaurants for their dates."

She went on, shaking her head. "Grabe naman kasi mambola 'yan si Mr. George. Kunyari daw magtatanan sila kasi obvious naman na ayaw ni Sir Will maging sila."

Jack flicked her arm. "Ay mare, that was before I heard muntik na'ng makabuntis si Mr. George nung girl na taga-Poveda."

My eyes widened even bigger than I imagined they could get. "What?"

He scoffed. "Naku, nung malaman ni Sir Will 'yon." He clicked his tongue. "Kulang na lang ipadala sa Canada si Miss Monica. Buti masunuring bata naman siya at napalayo din kay Mr. George."

"If you ask me, sinayang lang ni Mr. George yung job opportunity na binigay nila Sir," Jill added. "Ang sarap kaya mag-trabaho dito. Pero buti na lang napag-resign na siya."

"May mga tao talaga na hindi dapat pagkatiwalaan. Kung ako 'yun, pinakulong ko 'yon," Jack quipped, his lips curled in distaste. "Masyadong mabait talaga 'yang pamilyang Salcedo."

"Lalo sa si Sir Will," Jill pointed out. "Inaasikaso n'yang lahat. Alam mo talaga'ng back ka n'ya."

"Korek." Jack gave Jill a high-five.

I couldn't even shake my head in disbelief. I was frozen in shock. *Ho-ly shit.*

I had leafed through the files Will had provided for about ten minutes and then simply stared at them for a half-hour before Jill prompted if I wanted to use the photocopier machine. But I figured I'd seen enough.

I left Ayala Tower One—absolutely disoriented, completely frustrated, and utterly confused.

Ate Roweena was even more bewildered when I met up

with her at one of the restaurants in Ayala Triangle afterwards and told her what I had discovered about George.

She shook her head, her eyes wide, making her pause from cutting into the banoffee pie we were sharing. "Talaga ba? Hindi naman siguro kasing sama ng ganun. Baka naman exaggerated 'yang mga kwento."

I chuckled. Honestly, I was highly disappointed with my usual cynical self for having fallen for George's charming act but I wasn't surprised at all that Ate Roweena was still intent on thinking that maybe it was all just a big misunderstanding.

"Nakita ko 'yung papeles, Ate," I told her, sliding the dessert plate closer to me. "Nasa tama si Will." I stopped short, dropping my gaze. "Oh my gad, did I just say that?"

Ate Roweena bit her lip in mirth. "Maloloka sila Mommy kapag malaman nila 'yan."

I made a face. "Kailangan ba natin sabihin sa kanila?" My expression changed to skepticism. "Also, maniniwala kaya sila? Parang super baligtad ang opinions ng mga tao tungkol kay George at kay Will."

Ate Roweena was looking at me with an eager prompt. "Ano sa tingin mo?"

I pursed my lips, absently deconstructing the banoffee pie on the plate in consideration for a minute before finally resolving. "Wag na lang siguro. Anyway, malamang naman hindi na natin kailangan makita pa ya'ng dalawang 'yan, right?"

"Okayyy." Ate Roweena shrugged, concentrating on stirring her coffee. After another pause, she mused out loud, "I wonder kamusta na si Lance."

I snapped my gaze over to her but she didn't look up. I

resisted the urge to make a face, my chest suddenly feeling heavy because I knew all I could respond to her was, "Um, hindi ko siya nakita..."

23

Panahon

"O, eto, may isa pa." I whacked Stella's arm, motioning my mouth towards our house across the street while the two of us were hanging out at the chapel with my guitar and a big share bag of *Chippy*.

Stella looked up in eager anticipation even as she crunched on a mouthful.

Two gangly children were headed up to the gate that was swung half-open. Even in the dusk light, we could see that one of the kids was holding an empty tin can and a stick and the other one was holding a piece of wire with some bottlecaps threaded through it—which immediately began to rattle away.

"Sa may bahay, ang aming bati... Merry Christmas na maluwalhati—"

And as if on cue, from deep inside the house, we heard my dad's voice clearly sail out, *"Patawad na!"* followed by my mom's screech, "*Hoy, Nobyembre pa lang!*" all the while the dog had gone quite berserk, barking its head off.

My brother poked his head out from behind the wall, an already annoyed look on his face. "Hoy, ang aga n'yo naman!" he yelled out as he shooed the kids away. "Bumalik kayo sa Pasko!"

Bingka had run out of the gate to watch the prospective carollers, the string of Christmas lights she was holding trailing behind her on the ground and my brother yelled again, "Bingka! Bingka! Baka maapakan mo 'yung lights!" as he was attempting to hang said lights upon our roof.

Stella and I cracked up laughing at the uproar.

Then Stella turned to me, looking puzzled. "Bakit pala ngayon lang kayo naglalagay ng decorations?" she asked, licking her fingers. "Si Nick, mismong first of September, may Christmas tree na kami sa bahay."

She ticked off items from the same sticky fingers. "Sa ngayon, may belen na, may parol, nakakabit na 'yung lights, bumili pa nga ng inflatable Santa Claus at reindeer ang lolo mo. Mukha na kaming Paskuhan Village."

For some reason, Filipinos always associated the festive season with the ever-so-slight temperature drop nearing the end of the year. It meant three extra months of Christmas sales, Christmas shopping/spending, Christmas parties, and everything else in between. Hooray for commercialism.

I scoffed, giving Stella a pointed look. "Well, maraming mauutusan si Nick," I reminded her. "I mean, *kayo*," I amended with a grin and she rolled her eyes. "Kami dito, maski sumapit na ang *ber* months, busy pa rin sa trabaho."

We heard some more irritated yelling coming from the house.

"*Martin, nahanap mo ba 'yung parol?*"

"*Gusto n'yo ba hanapin ko 'yung parol o ikabit 'yung ilaw?*"

I shook my head in mirth. If I recalled correctly, our traditional ancient parol was going to need some major cosmetic repairs if it was going to be at all presentable to hang in the window as it was looking worse for wear when I had last seen it stashed in the backyard. We'd had it for over eight years, it having gone through several phases of re-covering while the main star-shaped skeleton stayed basically the same.

"Hindi ka ba tutulong?" Stella gestured to the house.

I gave her a smug look, leaning back against the chapel steps. "Aba, ako kaya nagtayo ng Christmas tree sa loob mag-isa kagabi. Buhul-buhol lahat nung decorations. Winalis ko pa yung lahat ng mga nalagas na dahon. Ang kalat ha."

"Sige na nga." Stella whacked my arm back. "Teka, teka, mabalik tayo sa usapan," she began, her eyebrows furrowed. "Tama ba 'yung pagkarinig ko sa sinabi mo?"

I pursed my lips and merely folded my arms across my chest in a silent 'yes.'

I wasn't at all surprised that even Stella had trouble believing the mindblowing/ridiculous/crazy story I had just told her. The said incident was nothing short of incredible. Suffice it to say, the look on her face said it all.

"Oh my god, what? That's so weird." She stopped short. "I mean not that it's impossible for guys to like you. But si Will?"

I gave her a meaningful look and moved to spin my index finger in circles around my ear.

Her eyebrows rose in a prompt, her eyes scandalous. "Anong sinabi mo?"

"Ano sa tingin mo?" I grimaced. "In any case, for sure, mag-ki-kick in din eventually yung 'katwiran' na sinasabi niya," I said, motioning air quotes with my fingers.

"Nakwento mo na kay Weena?"

I huffed in mocking. "Ha! Ayoko nga. In fact, mas mabuti pa siguro kalimutan mo na rin na sinabi ko sa'yo. Kunwari na lang hindi siya nangyari at all. Kaloka."

Aside from the fact that it was almost a surrealistic nightmare, I was also trying to avoid mentioning to Ate Roweena about Lance and his friends altogether, in case the conversation went around to 'why' our family was so unsuitable to match. I mean my sister was depressed enough.

I jumped in my seat as we heard more shouts coming from the house.

"*Hoy Carmina! 'Wag kang puro tambay lang diyan sa labas. Marami pang lilinisin.*"

"*Rene, tatawagin mo ba si Carmina para tumulong mag-ayos ng bahay o ano?*"

"*Gusto mo ba tawagin ko siya para tumulong o ano?*"

And Stella laughed again.

I rolled my eyes before hollering back, "Opo!" I cleared my throat, starting to stand and dusting crumbs off my jeans. "Sige na nga. Tara na." I picked up my guitar.

Stella began to gather up her stuff, grabbing the half-empty *Chippy* bag as she stood. Her eyes lit up as she spotted Ate Roweena walking down the street and turning the corner. "Ay, nandyan na rin si Weena."

Ate Roweena saw us by the chapel steps and gave us a wave even as she headed straight for the house.

Stella and I followed suit and overheard my mom's greeting, "O, Rowena. Ngayon ka pa lang natapos sa trabaho?"

But before my sister could respond, Mom spotted Stella and me and my mom's eyes lit up. "O Stella!" she greeted with a big smile. "Long time no see ha, iha. Kamusta pala yung honeymoon mo? Saan ulit kayo nagpunta ni Nick?"

Stella gave her a smile back. "Ay, sa El Nido po, sa Palawan. Okay naman po." She nodded, her eyes shining. "Ang ganda po nung resort!"

From what Stella had told me, the resort they had stayed at was like a paradise on Earth. You barely had to lift a finger. Everything was done for you. Not to mention, the food and the views were all amazing. Palawan sounded like such a magical place where anything could happen. Nakaka-in love.

"Aba, siguro nga naman at pagka-mahal-mahal ng mga resort na 'yan, 'di ba?" my mom commented with a haughty look on her face as she took off the covers on the throw pillows on the couch to swap them out for Christmas ones. "Kailangan yata may kilala ka muna'ng congressman bago ka makapunta sa mga lugar na ganyan." She let out a big sigh. "Kung ako lang, hindi naman ako talagang mahilig sa beach."

My dad and I exchanged amused looks knowing full well there was no way on Earth my mom actually meant that.

"Ayaw n'yo doon, mga anak? Wala tayong kailangan gawin kundi humilata lang sa beach buong araw. Kung ako, okay ako dun," Dad mused as he took one end of the string of lights and headed to the door to help Martin.

Bingka was trying to keep Basti from chewing on the the Christmas tree skirt on the floor. "Daddy, kailan po tayo pupunta sa Palawan?"

My dad cracked a wry smile. "Pag manalo sa lotto si Daddy, Bingka."

My mom shot him a sharp look. "Hoy Rene, may pera ka pang-lotto? Akin na 'yan. Sayang."

Stella and I met each other's gazes and laughed before she spoke up, "Sige, teka Armi, kailangan ko na umuwi. Kailangan ko pa'ng ayusin 'yung papeles ng joint insurance at 'yung mga titulo."

"Tsk tsk." I shook my head. "Ayan ang napapala. Nag-asa-asawa ka pa kasi."

"Loko-loko." Stella stuck her tongue out at me before she turned to leave with a wave at everyone. "Ah, sige po, Tita, Tito. Uuwi na po ako."

"Ay, sige, anak," my mom bid her with a brief wave before going back to her throw pillows.

"Ingat sa pag-drive!" my dad called out.

"Bye, Stella." I mocked a salute and stood by the gate to watch until the car drove away and disappeared around the corner. I was coming back inside to put my guitar away when, as she tended to do, my mother started her litany.

"Mabuti pa si Stella, nakapag-asawa na ng mayaman," Mom remarked with another big sigh as she fluffed the throw pillows, her tone as though she was talking to herself but loud enough that everyone could hear. "Samantalang yung anak ko—ang bait-bait, ang tali-talino, ang ganda-ganda. Naiwan lang basta ng manliligaw. Sayang talaga!"

I glanced up at Ate Roweena who had just come back out to the living room to help out after getting changed out of her work clothes.

I made a face when her expression instantly changed as she overheard. Our mom had barely spoken to her about anything else in the last few weeks.

"Hay nako, kawawa naman talaga 'yung anak ko. At 'yang Lance na 'yan. Akala mo ang bait-bait. Akala mo honorable. Manloloko rin pala. Sana ma-flat lahat ng gulong ng lahat ng kotse n'ya. Wag na siyang bumalik."

I wrinkled my nose but didn't say anything. The way Mom was talking, it was as though she had never fawned all over him to begin with. As though there was absolutely no redeeming his character.

It was difficult to hear especially for me since I knew that Lance was actually the great guy that we had met and known and liked. I could only guess what Ate Roweena was feeling about it.

"Adel naman," my dad chided. "Hayaan mo na 'yung tao. Hindi naman natin alam ang buong kwento."

"Hay. Kung anuman. Pero mabuti na rin lumayas na sila at hindi na rin natin kailangan makita yung suplado niyang kaibigan. Kung makatingin eh akala mo siya na ang pinaka-magaling sa mundo. Maski gaano sila kayaman, isumpa na natin ang mga bwiset na 'yan. Salcedo. Ortega. Pare-pareho silang lahat."

My stomach churned and I met Ate's gaze again. My parents just didn't understand. I also figured that we were probably right not to have told everyone what we had discovered about George's and Will's character reversal since it looked like people's opinions of them were too far established to be able to be changed.

"Kukunin ko lang 'yung parol sa likod bahay," Ate Roweena volunteered.

Concerned, I followed her to the kitchen. "Okay ka lang, Ate?"

Ate Roweena gave me a small smile. "Oo naman," she assured. "Tapos na 'yun, diba? Wala na tayong magagawa." She shrugged. "Anyway, kinalimutan ko na rin siya. Lalaki lang naman 'yon. Marami pa namang iba diyan."

My forehead creased as I tried to read into her tone.

But she sighed first and dropped her gaze. "Nakakalungkot lang kasi..." She shook her head, pausing for a moment. "Akala ko talaga..."

Then she just let out another big sigh and dismissed with a wave. "Ay, hayaan mo na 'yun. I'm over him na." She met my gaze with another serene smile and a nod. "Okay na ako. Promise."

I made a face as I watched her expression. All I could do was pat her back in consolation, my heart aching even more because if I told her the actual truth of it, I was sure it would just make things worse.

24

Pasalubong

The next evening was cause for some excitement as my OFW Ninang Amy was arriving from overseas.

Interestingly, my Ninang Amy had been born only five years before my Ate Roweena. As such, Ninang Amy was actually more of another elder sister to me than an aunt, much less an actual godmother.

Since it was fairly common for Filipinos to have large families, it was not uncommon to have a large age gap between siblings, particularly between the eldest and the youngest children, which in my mom's family's case was thirteen years.

Ninang Amy was the most fortunate one of them all. Mom had worked several jobs to be able to send her to college, after which Ninang Amy was able to get work in Australia where she had been living for the last decade or so. She hadn't been back to the country for five years.

I waved at the black Subaru SUV as it pulled up to park

right in front of our house. "Mommy! Ito na sila Ninang Amy."

My mom paused from drying plates in the kitchen and turned around with a big sigh. "Ay, sa wakas." She waved my dad over and they both headed to the gate.

Mom came up to kiss Ninang Amy's cheek in greeting as soon as she stepped out of the car. "O, bakit ngayon lang kayo? Na-late ba 'yung flight n'yo?"

"Kamusta, Ate?" Ninang Amy gave her a nod.

At her prompt, my mom moaned out loud. "Nako, tag-hirap tayo ngayon, Amy. Puro perwisyo at abala at ang daming kailangan gawin. Sobrang nakaka-stress. Samantalang, hindi naman ako damayan ng pamilya ko. Buti na lang hindi ako mareklamong tao."

I met my dad's highly amused gaze from behind my mom and couldn't help a chuckle.

Then Bingka's greeting chimed from behind me. "Tita Amy!"

"O, Bingka. Hi Martin, Armi." Ninang Amy beamed at us before turning to the tall, blond guy who had stepped out of the car behind her. "Ngapala, Ate, everyone, this is Roger Parnell."

Martin craned his neck to have a clear look. My dad holding Basti on his leash also gave the guy a curious once-over.

It was our first time meeting her boyfriend. Not to mention it was *his* first time to be visiting this wonderful tropical developing (not third-world) country called "The Republic of the Philippines."

"G'day. Good to meet you all," was Roger's accented greeting. He gave my dad's hand a vigorous shake.

"Welcome, welcome, Roger," my dad responded with a nod and a big smile as he gestured into the house. "Pasok kayo. Sorry it's hot. That's the Philippines," he added with a nervous chuckle.

My mom was giving Roger an awed sort of look, as though she had never seen someone so tall in her life. "Ay, hello. How are you? Did you have traffic coming here?"

Ninang Amy answered for him. "Ay Ate, ang daming tao. Grabe talaga ang traffic sa airport."

"Malapit na kasi mag-Pasko. Uwian na lahat," my dad relayed as we all shuffled into the house.

My mom fussed over her sister. "Bakit nag-renta pa kayo ng kotse? Sinabi ko sa'yo pwede n'yo naman hiramin 'yung taxi."

"Okay na, Ate. Ayaw naman namin maka-abala sa inyo. Alam ko kailangan ni Kuya 'yung taxi." She gestured towards the car again. "'Yung mga kahon pala na pasalubong nasa trunk, sandali." She turned to Roger again. "Babe, can you get the boxes from the boot?"

My dad rushed to help, waving Martin over to help Roger unload the trunk. "Martin, halika."

"Yehey! Pasalubong! Pasalubong!" Bingka cheered, jumping up and down.

Ninang Amy directed Martin and my dad to unload the boxes of *pasalubong* from the trunk of their rental SUV. Bingka eagerly peeked into each box as they were opened one by one in the living room.

I was in the kitchen, mixing up a huge pitcher of iced tea for everyone so I only caught fragments of the conversations.

"'Yung isang kahon diyan, nandyan 'yung cheese na pinabili n'yo."

"Alin po dito 'yung Christmas gift ko?"

"Rog, can you please find the smoker manuka wood chips? 'Yun 'yung pinabilin ni Tita Beth na pang-barbecue."

"Kailan tayo pupunta ng Duty Free?"

"Kailangan ba talaga natin magpunta ulit ng Duty Free every time?"

I brought out the tray of juice glasses and set it on the table in the living room. I noticed that after unloading the boxes, "Tito" Roger, having gotten the wi-fi password, seemed content to sit in one corner with his attention fully on his cellphone while Ninang Amy caught up with the rest of us, telling stories.

I handed him his glass of iced tea since it looked like he didn't want to move at all and he thanked me with a brief smile before I went to sit on the couch on the other side of Ninang Amy.

"Nakabili ka nung beef steak na sinabi ko, Amy?" my mom was asking.

I thought I saw Ninang Amy roll her eyes before she responded to my mom's question. "Ate, mahirap magdala n'un."

"Pwede naman ilagay sa chiller or styrofoam box na may yelo. Okay lang 'yon."

"Matagal 'yung flight, Ate. Mahirap na. Sayang lang kung mabulok or kumalat."

"Sayang naman 'yung baggage allowance mo. Binayaran mo rin 'yon," Mom said matter-of-factly with a tone of authority. "Palibhasa mayaman ka kasi. So hindi mo iniisip ang mga 'yan."

Ninang Amy sighed in exasperation. "Ate naman, sinabi ko na sa inyo dati, hindi po lahat ng OFW mayaman. Dollars nga ang kita namin, pero dollars din ang gasta. At mas mahal ang mga bagay sa Australia. Lalo na ang tax!"

I could tell from the expression on my mom's face that she wasn't entirely convinced.

It was one of those ingrained cultural Pinoy myths that were very likely going to be difficult to debunk. It was also for sure another manifestation of the generation gap between the two of them.

As far as I was concerned, Ninang Amy and I had a standing agreement in terms of her being my godmother. Gifts were appreciated but absolutely not required. We were both capable working adults after all.

"Tao po!" Ate Roweena was outside the gate, having just arrived home from work. Basti jerked with a start, scrambling over to bark at her arrival.

"Uy, andyan na rin si Ate." I jumped up from my seat to go and open the gate for her.

When Ate Roweena entered the living room, she saw the new arrivals. "Uy, Tita Amy, welcome back!" she greeted with a big smile as she took off her shoes by the door.

Ninang Amy turned to Ate Roweena. "O, Weena, kamusta na?" Then her expression changed almost instantly to an eager smile. "Uy, kamusta pala 'yung boyfriend mo? Na-kwento sa'kin ng mommy mo before. Ang pogi daw at mabait."

My eyes widened and I tried to shake my head at Ninang Amy from behind Ate Roweena to make her stop talking but she didn't see me in time.

And unfortunately, my mom replied before Ate Roweena

could. "Hay nako, Amy. Kalimutan mo na 'yon. Iniwan na kami'ng lahat. Hindi na daw babalik. Mabuti na rin. Mga demonyo. Mga demonyo silang lahat."

Ate Roweena grimaced for a second before she put on a small forced smile. "Um, magbibihis lang muna ako," she said, heading towards the hallway.

I watched her leave with a helpless sigh of my own before I slumped into the armchair by the doorway.

Ninang Amy looked puzzled at everyone's reaction to her question. "Ay, ano ba'ng nangyari?"

And my mom's eyes lit up just as they usually did whenever the opportunity for *chismis* came up and she shifted up closer to Ninang Amy on the couch. "Hay nako, Amy. Halika dito. Ikukwento ko sa'yo ang lahat—"

Martin was sitting on the floor, busy tinkering with the new drone flyer that Ninang Amy had bought him when his phone beeped loudly with a message alert and he picked up his phone to read it. "Ayos. Nag-organize ng outing this weekend ang tropa." He glanced up at my mom and dad. "Okay po, Mommy, Daddy? Sasama po ako ha."

"Hoy, anong outing 'yan? Saan? Sinong kasama?" Mom prompted, waving him away towards my Dad to sort it out while she eagerly leaned in to continue to gossip with Ninang Amy.

Martin looked at Dad. "Sa Antipolo po. Kasama si George at 'yung ibang mga kabarkada niya."

The mention of the name made me sit upright, alarm bells already ringing in my head, and I tossed Martin a pointed look. "Hoy, tumino-tino ka nga. 'Wag kang puro gala. Lalo na kasama 'yang George na 'yan," I said, trying to be careful what I exposed.

But Martin just rolled his eyes as he stood up, gathering up his new toys. "Ate naman. Dahil lang hindi bumalik si George sa'yo maski break na sila ng GF niya, 'wag ka naman bitter," he taunted.

I gave Martin my death stare but he just laughed and disappeared into the hall, heading for his room.

He obviously didn't understand the gravity of the situation. Nor could I tell him.

I blew out a breath and turned to my dad instead, aghast. "Daddy, papayagan n'yo ba 'yan?"

"O bakit, ano ba'ng problema?" he asked, sounding puzzled, although he was paying more attention to the TV about to start *Ang Probinsyano*.

I guessed it was uncharacteristic of me to act like a concerned older sister all of a sudden.

I groaned inwardly, trying to think of how to explain without actually explaining. "I mean, hindi kaya delikado? Hindi natin kilala lahat ang kasama nila. Baka kung ano pa ang mangyari. Mahirap na."

"Armi, matanda na rin 'yang kapatid mo," my dad reasoned, casting me a dismissive glance. "At saka hindi naman sila masyadong lalayo. Tutal, kung ano man ang mangyari, isipin mo na lang na 'learning experience' 'yan kay Martin," he concluded as he reached for the remote to turn up the TV volume.

Under normal circumstances, I would have no problem letting Martin join this type of outing as he had done so in the past. But knowing what I now knew about George, all I had was a bad feeling in the pit of my stomach.

I could only make a face in displeasure as, save for the truth, I knew there was nothing else I could say to change my dad's mind.

Ate Roweena trudged back into the living room and Ninang Amy's eyes lit up. "Uy, Weena, Armi, girls." She glanced over at me as well. "I'm meeting some friends from my old choir sa Makati. Umuwi 'yung dating conductor nami'ng si Jun back from the States. They're having a reunion of sorts. Baka kumain kami sa labas. Taralets, bagets!" She waved to beckon.

I laughed at her archaic slang.

But Ate Roweena heaved a sigh, merely giving Ninang Amy another small smile and waving us away. "Sige, kayo na lang muna. Napagod ako sa trabaho today eh."

Ninang Amy frowned. "Ay ganoon. Sige na nga. Pahinga ka na lang," she called out then turned to me with a firm look. "Ikaw, Armi. Sama ka na ha," she said like I wasn't allowed to say no.

25

Food for thought

Did I mention that Christmas was my favorite time of year? There's just nothing as magical and nostalgia-inducing as the smell of *castañas* actually roasting in a plaza square and the sight of all the little *karitelas* lining the street, peddling their *bibingka* and steamed rice cakes, each stand lit with a single light bulb in the darkness of the cool-ish evening air.

Not to mention, nothing ever made drab old churches look as good as being covered in Christmas decorations—Santuario de San Antonio Church being absolutely no exception.

That evening, every facet of the church facade was outlined with Christmas lights and classy wreaths; every archway inside laden with green boughs, red ribbons, and more lights, and the dozen or so giant hanging chandeliers of fake candelabras were dressed with festive green garlands and big shiny red balls.

I spent most of the mass smiling like a four-year-old up

at all the decorations, enjoying the ambiance, and I was still engrossed in the peace and serenity of my little Christmas wonderland that during the closing blessing, I completely didn't hear the guy at the lectern announce something.

"Tonight's advent mass is sponsored by Mr. and Mrs. Fernando Salcedo."

I only snapped to attention when Ninang Amy elbowed me to shuffle down the pew once the service was over and it was time to leave. But while the rest of the crowd headed down the aisle towards the church exit, Ninang Amy tugged Roger's arm towards the area beside the altar where the church choir was.

I lagged behind since I wasn't at all acquainted with the church choir and I only watched from afar as Ninang Amy greeted several of her friends there with enthusiastic hugs and squealy *beso-besos.*

By the time I arrived near the altar myself, Ninang Amy and Roger were saying hello to the mass celebrant.

"Mano po, Father Roly." Ninang Amy put the priest's hand to her forehead as a sign of respect.

"O, Amy. Long time no see," Father Roly began. "Hello, Roger. Nice to meet you."

I watched as Roger made pleasantries with the priest. Roger had been really chatty in the car on the way over but as soon as we were in the vicinity of other people, he was like a completely different person. Then again it was his first time in this new culture and new environment and new language.

Ninang Amy gestured towards the door. "O, hatid na po namin kayo, Father. Saan po ba kayo pupunta?" she proposed as we all walked out of the church to go back to where we parked the car.

Father Roly smiled in appreciation. "Ah, maraming sala-mat naman, iha, sige. Diyan lang sa Narra Avenue." Then he beckoned to us. "Sumama na rin kayo sa pakain. Simple lang naman. Tutal choir ka rin dati at malapit lang din—"

My eyes had lit up at the word *pakain*. I glanced up and saw the same look on Ninang Amy's face.

Then Father Roly went on. "—diyan kina Mrs. Salcedo."

And I stopped short, blinking at the name.

Ninang Amy's eyes narrowed. "Salcedo? Why does that last name sound familiar?"

Father Roly nodded. "Ah, sila ang annual sponsor ng advent mass. You know, Monica Salcedo is one of the most talented singers in the choir now. Usually nga, nag-aattend din sila Will at Monica nitong misa." He paused in thought. "Pero parang hindi ko sila nakita kanina."

We arrived at the SUV and when Roger opened the door for Father Roly, Ninang Amy yanked me back to whisper hoarsely, "Salcedo? 'Yan ba 'yung suplado na na-kwento sa'kin ng Mommy mo? 'Yun daw daig pa si Senyora Santibañez sa ka-sungitan na palibhasa kasi'ng yaman ni Henry Sy, sobrang yabang, at sana mabulok na lang sa impyerno ang kaluluwa niya at nilang lahat?"

I nodded, resisting the urge to laugh at my mother's colorful words of description before giving Ninang Amy a meaningful look. "Oh, yeah. Uuwi na tayo, right?" I told her, my statement more like a directive than a question.

Ninang Amy gave me a pout. "Aww, tara na, Armi. I need

my *puto bumbong* fix. Akala mo ba ba't ako umuwi sa Pilipinas? Siyempre para kumain. Maski sandali lang tayo dun, dali na," she urged, yanking on my arm.

Father Roly was still going on in the car like he was used to giving sermons. "Actually, nagpahanda lang siguro si Mrs. Salcedo. Out of town yata ang buong mag-pamilya this week at baka pati sa abroad silang lahat mag-Pasko. Siguro binilin lang kay Pilar itong pakain."

At that, Ninang Amy shot me an instant eyebrow-raised expectant look. "You mean, wala 'yung pamilya?" She elbowed me in the ribs, mouthing 'Tara!'

I rolled my eyes. I was recalling an earlier account of how this house was supposedly at least twice bigger than Lance Ortega's already giant new house and my eyebrows furrowed in almost skepticism. How big could it actually, really be?

Honestly, curiosity got the better of me. Also Ninang Amy's relentless nagging.

Well, kung out of town sila anyway... I shrugged in resignation.

Ninang Amy turned to give me a big satisfied grin and a high-five. "Ayos."

We weren't even there yet and I could already tell which house it was.

It had to be the biggest one on the street. The house whose entire front was covered in Christmas lights and over a dozen multi-colored parols of all shapes and sizes. The street front was also full of fancy parked cars.

Yup, this was definitely the right place.

I was stunned into silence as we rolled up to the side of the house. The lot was also a compound like Lance's house and it was definitely about twice as long. Or at least what we could see from the street was. It was probably even bigger inside just as everyone had attested, despite the frontage being simple—a three-car garage and a varnished wooden door with a wreath on it just beyond the wide-open gate.

The housekeeper Ate Pilar met us at the door. She was an older lady with a friendly face but she moved with an air of purpose and efficiency. I could imagine she had probably worked for the family for a long, long time, and was a highly trusted member of the household staff.

"Welcome po, Father, Sir, Ma'am," she beckoned us over.

As soon as we stepped inside, I took a deep breath in awe.

The living room had a high ceiling and there was a wide staircase at the far end. A delicate crocheted throw hung over the leather couch beside some bean bags which matched the area rug.

Every corner of the room was adorned with Christmas decorations—green garlands, wreaths, holly, but not the usual tacky kind you see in malls or everywhere else. The accents were tasteful, not too much, and not too gaudy either.

The room was like a beautiful, glittery, but somehow also cozy home. The huge Christmas tree in the middle of the room was almost as high as the ceiling. It was already surrounded by a pile of tidily-wrapped presents. The entire place looked like it came straight out of a Christmas edition Home & Décor magazine.

Ate Pilar led the three of us through the living room towards what she called the 'conservatory' on the other side of the house where they were entertaining tonight's guests.

Ninang Amy immediately began chatting up Ate Pilar as we walked through the house. 'Kamusta po. Ang ganda ng bahay. Ang ganda ng decorations. Matagal na po ba kayo dito. May puto bumbong po ba.'

I remained as silent as Tito Roger.

We passed a hallway of pictures and almost involuntarily, I stopped short when I glimpsed a familiar face on the wall.

Will's.

The framed pictures included his graduation picture from Ateneo and from AIM. There was also a picture of him accepting some type of certificate in front of a big sign 'Wharton School of Business. Philadelphia, Pennsylvania.' There were also more formal portraits of Will with his parents probably taken at some expensive studio.

Ninang Amy glanced back and noticed me having stopped. She walked back towards me to look at the pictures herself. "Wow, Ate Pilar," she breathed. "'Yan ba si William?" She turned to me. "Armi, hindi mo naman na-mention, ang pogi pala ni Will."

My mouth went dry. "Um..."

Ate Pilar turned to me with eyebrows raised. "Magkakilala po kayo ni Sir Will, Ma'am?"

I managed a weak smile. "Konti lang po."

Ate Pilar looked very proud. "Hindi po ba sobrang artistahin si Sir Will? Talo pa n'ya 'yung mga *oppa* sa TV," she remarked.

Ninang Amy giggled and elbowed Ate Pilar. "Naks, Ate Pilar naman, up-to-date pala kayo sa K-drama!"

Ate Pilar went on like she had been switched on. "At hindi lang gwapo, napakabait na amo ni Sir Will, maski nung bata pa siya. Napaka-matulungin. Napaka-disente. Pati si Miss Monica, napaka-mapagkumbaba, napaka-talentado. Kunsabagay, nag-mana ang mga anak sa mga magulang nila. Lalo si Sir Will, napaka-responsable, napaka-maalalahanin."

Ninang Amy shot me a discreet sideways look of disbelief. Of course, as far as she had been told, Will Salcedo was the devil incarnate so I could fully understand her skepticism.

I simply pursed my lips in response as my own brain was about to explode.

26

Langit

Ninang Amy didn't comment on it further or attempt to refute the statement. Instead, she just prompted Ate Pilar, "Wala ba sila today?"

"Ay, madalas po silang wala," Ate Pilar replied with a rueful smile. "Kung hindi lang nga po dahil sa trabaho ay siguro lagi'ng nandito si Sir Will sa bahay. Madalas kasi'ng wala sila Sir Nan. Si Sir Will na ang namamahala. Sabi nga niya, maski nakapag-abroad na daw siya, ito pa rin ang pinaka-paborito niya'ng lugar sa mundo."

She shook her head. "Kung sabagay, hindi rin magtatagal, siya rin ang magmamana. Mabuti na rin. Umaasa rin kami'ng lahat na makapag-asawa na siya ng mabuti para naman medyo mag-hinay-hinay na siya sa kaka-trabaho. Napaka-sipag na bata," she finished with another shake of her head, her tone full of pride.

My face had been twisted in a grimace for like ten minutes

almost in disbelief of what Ate Pilar was saying. It was true my opinion of Will was a bit uneven since I found out the truth about what had happened between him and George but platitudes of Will's virtues were all still very confusing to hear.

Gusto kita.

I shivered involuntarily at the fragment of memory, my frown deepening as I also recalled what my response had been. I groaned under my breath in self-loathing.

Ang bitch mo, Armi.

Ate Pilar led us past the hallway and I could see a handful of people gathered in the conservatory up ahead.

"Uy, andyan na si Rochelle." Ninang Amy's eyes lit up as she spotted her choir friends and she rushed down the hall and across the room, tugging on Roger's hand as she went along.

I was going to follow suit when I saw something out of the corner of my eye and I turned towards a room with the door ajar. Curious, I peeked through the gap in the door and my eyes widened, already in bewilderment. "Anong...?"

Several guitars hung on the wall and were propped on display stands. There were two Fender Stratocasters, a Gibson Les Paul, several Fender offsets, a couple of acoustic guitars, as well as some vintage and rare-looking guitars. They were all so freaking shiny.

Ate Pilar noticed me by the door. "'Yan po 'yung music room," she relayed. "Karamihan po 'yung guitar collection ni Sir Will." Then she waved me back towards the conservatory where everyone else had gone. "This way po yung pakain, ma'am."

I had trouble dragging myself away from the door. Will Salcedo collected guitars? *No F'ing way!*

When I caught up to Ninang Amy, she turned to me with a wide-eyed, ridiculously impressed look on her face. "Grabe, ang ganda ng bahay!" she hissed. "Sayang naman talaga suplado 'yung may-ari."

I could only look at her, still sort of dumbfounded.

But then Ninang Amy took a sip of her fruit punch and added, quite offhandedly, "Although, 'wag ka. Nakaka-pogi points 'yung bahay."

I looked up, only then taking in the full ambiance of my impressive surroundings.

Outside the glass windows, there were two pools and a Jacuzzi beside a garden with rolling green Bermuda grass. There were spotlights and *capiz* lanterns in amongst the trees and flowers, giving the entire garden an ethereal glow.

The lawn was easily twice the size of Nick's Tita's. There was a small gazebo all the way across to the end of the property also adorned in Christmas lights and mock icicles. To its left, a *belen* had been staged between some shrubs under an actual constructed *nipa hut*.

It was like 9 p.m. but everything was bathed in light, in part from the twinkling Christmas lights that had been strung everywhere.

Everything looked so magical and beautiful and posh.

I was quite unnerved by the sheer everything of everything. I spotted Ate Pilar by the corner and promptly approached her to ask, "Um, excuse me, saan po 'yung CR?"

"Ah, dito po, ma'am."

I blew out a breath as I strode down the hall in the

direction that Ate Pilar pointed. This house was just something else. And everything I was finding out about Will was highly disconcerting.

On my way back from the toilet (which by the way looked like a hotel bathroom with all the fancy soaps, I almost thought I would fill in a satisfaction survey on the way out), I passed a glass bookcase with an assortment of sports trophies displayed on it—most of it inscribed to one William Salcedo and I was shaking my head in utter incredulity as I turned the corner.

I almost jumped out of my skin at the sight of him.

Will looked just as shocked, his mouth dropping open, his hands frozen where they were. That was, halfway from unbuttoning his shirt.

I swallowed, looking him up and down. His hair was still a bit tousled and I could see the bare top half of his chest. *Oh shit.*

I flushed red and turned my head. "Umm...sorry!" I put my hand up to block my eyes. "Nag-CR lang ako. I didn't know— may tao pala dito."

He turned his back to button his shirt up again and ran his hand through his hair a few times even as he spoke, "Ah. That's fine. Um. Kasama ka ba doon sa church choir?"

"Y-yeah." I nodded, still trying not to look at him. "I mean yung Ninang ko. I mean nandito yung Ninang ko from Australia so she's...visiting. Uh, sorry talaga! Sabi ni Father Roly, wala daw kayong mag-pamilya."

"Uh, kararating ko lang." I heard him shift on his feet. "Um, I just—magbibihis lang ako. Okay?"

"Sure, sure!" I waved him away. "Sorry ulit." I whirled around and half-ran back to the conservatory. *Oh my gaaaad!*

Ninang Amy saw me rushing back and noticed the look on my face. "O, anong nangyari sa'yo?"

I pursed my lips, still shaking my head.

Not that I could have convinced Ninang Amy to turn down free food but I really *shouldn't* have come to this house tonight! Who knew what Will could be thinking? Given our last encounter, he was probably thinking I was now trying to stalk him or something!

"Hindi pa ba tayo uuwi?" I urged, pulling on her arm, looking around furtively. "Dali na. Ibaon mo na 'yung mga bibingka."

"Sandali lang!" Ninang Amy waved me away as she went for the buffet table.

"Armi!"

I stopped and looked over.

Will strode down the hallway towards us. He had finished getting changed and was wearing a dark blue blazer over a crisp white Chinese-collared shirt. His hair was neatly combed, his bangs hanging over his eyes.

When I met his gaze, his mouth curved into a smile, the Christmas lights twinkling in his eyes.

I swallowed hard again, my pulse already racing. For some reason, it was now damn near impossible to ignore how hot he was. I didn't even know how I'd managed to do it for so long since having met him.

He stopped in front of me.

But I was having trouble making my mouth work.

Will tilted his head to peer at the strange expression on my face, his forehead already creasing. "Hi."

It took *a lot* of effort to drag my gaze away from him but after a moment, I pointed towards the pool and around us in an attempt to focus on something else. "Um...ang ganda ng bahay n'yo."

His eyes lit up, looking pleased. "You like the house?"

I chuckled nervously, looking anywhere else but him. "Sino kaya'ng hindi?"

"But I know *you* don't take things for granted," Will pointed out, his tone wry. "So that means more."

In spite of myself, I couldn't help a glance up at him. His smile was absolutely mesmerizing.

"A-hem."

I jumped at Ninang Amy's hand on my arm and I turned to see her and Roger behind me.

They were holding plates heaped with rice cakes. She gave me a pointed prompting look and I snapped to attention. "Ah! Ninang, Tito, this is Will Salcedo po." I gestured towards Will.

Will gave them a respectful nod. "It's nice to meet you po." He turned to me. "Sabi po ni Armi, you're visiting from Australia? When did you arrive?"

"We just arrived earlier this evening," Ninang Amy answered.

"Wow, you must be exhausted," Will remarked, glancing from Ninang Amy to Roger with an impressed look.

A little weirded out, I watched Will being uncharacteristically polite and charming to my family. I distinctly remembered a comment he'd made about how allegedly embarrassing he thought we all were.

Though I had to admit I was grateful Will wasn't trying to humiliate any of us by pointing it out.

And to Ninang Amy and Roger's credit, they weren't staring open-mouthed at the luxury around us or trying to fill their bags with the free food. They were relatively cultured people who had been living abroad for about a decade and been out in the wide, wide world mixing with a lot more diverse society than this.

"Well, we didn't want to waste any time on this visit," Ninang Amy was saying. "It's Rog's first time in the Philippines and it might be too ambitious but I wanted him to see everything."

"Well, have you been to Hacienda Salcedo?" Will's eyebrows rose in suggestion. "It's a prime tourist destination and has a worldwide reputation for showcasing Filipino culture. Christmas season there is the best."

"I've heard of it." Ninang Amy nodded, glancing up to meet Roger's gaze in a prompt and he nodded too. "I think it was on our list of places to go, wasn't it?"

Will's eyes lit up. "Great! I was planning to take my sister there tomorrow. If you're not too jetlagged, why don't we all meet up? May kailangan din akong asikasuhin. But I'd love to personally take you all on a tour."

Naturally, his invitation was met with enthusiastic grins of agreement from Ninang Amy and Roger.

Will peered at my face again, his expression almost tentative. "I'm sure Monica would love to meet you. If that's okay."

I almost held my breath but I managed to crack a smile and simply nodded.

***

27

Lupa

Unsurprisingly, everything was too hot for Roger.

The hotel room. The house. The car. The gas station. The Jollibee at the gas station. And every other rest stop along the ninety-kilometer road on the way to Hacienda Salcedo the next day.

Ninang Amy had to distract him by pointing out several definitive local sights—the dwindling rice fields along the SLEX, the distant view of Enchanted Kingdom, the even more distant view of Mount Banahaw.

I already couldn't sit still in the car the entire drive down, being wholly preoccupied. My mind was racing with ridiculous thoughts that took a lot of effort to shut up.

Last night's meeting with Will was still blowing my mind. Why had he been so nice to us? To me? If I were in his shoes, I would totally hate me right now. Had he even forgotten the last thing I'd said to him?

Maski nung unang time kita na-meet, I knew there was seriously absolutely no way I was ever going to like you.

EVER.

My cheeks flushed red with mortification right before my heart began to pound as I remembered something else. Again.

Gusto kita.

I took a deep breath. No way. That was super long ago. He'd definitely gotten over that by now for sure.

Regardless, I was decided to be nice to him today. If he could exhibit some normal human decency, so could I.

He was probably just doing the professional thing and being courteous to new tourists who might bring him business in the future.

So bakit ka gusto ipakilala sa sister niya?

I muffled my groan of confusion and anxiety. Sitting in the car, I had nothing else to do except think and think and think, driving myself close to crazy.

Between that and Roger's constant moaning about how the car air conditioning wasn't set high enough, I was relieved when we finally turned down the unsealed road leading into the parking lot at our destination.

As we walked into the open-air native *nipa* hut lobby, a few of the staff dressed in the native *baro't saya* handed out ice-cold welcome drinks which Ninang Amy and most notably Roger eagerly grabbed.

I shook my head in mirth.

Hacienda Salcedo was eight hundred hectares of a self-contained working coconut plantation and lush nature reserve. There was a heritage museum, a buffet restaurant, and a water park.

I had been here once before but only on the basic tour, of course, and it wasn't Christmas at the time.

I marveled up at all the beautiful braided parols lining the entrance archway and hanging from the beams amidst the woven basket light fixtures and wooden ceiling fans. Native carvings flanked the little souvenir shop in the corner peddling even more crafts for tourists—*buri* hats and *pamaypays*.

I couldn't help a wondrous smile.

Christmas season here *was* the best.

I spotted Will immediately. Only because he stood out. But I would probably have had no trouble picking him out of any crowd.

He was speaking to a pretty girl wearing tailored shorts, a sleeveless blouse, and classy thread drop earrings. But it wasn't hard to guess who she was because Will was looking at her like an adoring, protective Kuya.

Bright and cheerful, Monica saw me first and she almost jumped, her ponytail bouncing. "She's here!"

Will turned to look and when he met my gaze, it was like his whole face lit up even with only the ghost of a smile on his lips.

It took some effort to suppress my big idiot smile. My face flushed again and I was afraid everyone could hear my heart pounding as we approached them.

Homaygahd. Chill ka lang, girl!

I pulled myself together and managed to quickly introduce Ninang Amy and Roger.

"And this is my sister, Monica." Will made a sort of grand sweeping sideways motion with his arm.

Monica beamed at me. "I'm so glad you made it! I've been

looking forward to finally meeting you in forever. Kuya's told me so much about you."

My gaze darted up to Will in wary concern. "Hala."

Will actually had to stifle back his chuckle. But he merely shook his head before gesturing towards reception. "Sabihan ko lang sila na we're all here."

Monica watched her brother stroll across the lobby before she turned back to me with a smile, glancing back at Ninang Amy and Roger. "Okay po ba 'yung drive down? Sana hindi kayo na-traffic."

I returned her smile. "Okay lang naman."

Roger gestured to the Nikon camera strapped around Monica's neck. "Is that a DSLR?"

Monica nodded. "Oh, yeah."

Ninang Amy's eyes lit up too. "Ah, Roger is also into photography."

"I have a similar one at home with a few zoom lenses," Roger supplied. "I've actually been thinking of getting an upgrade. My camera is over five years old."

"You must be really good," Ninang Amy remarked. "Parang magandang camera 'yan a."

"Ay, no po." She shook her head. "I only mentioned to Kuya na I wanted to try to get into photography and he bought me this."

"Well, that's a D850," Roger supplied, looking impressed. "It's a really good professional camera."

Monica's cheeks reddened and she dropped her gaze. "Yes, it is. Sabi ko kay Kuya masyadong mahal," she explained. "Honestly, I probably won't even be any good but Kuya thinks I'll be the next Annie Leibovitz."

Surprised by her humility, I furrowed my eyebrows. Somehow I had a sneaking suspicion that she was probably exactly as talented as I had been led to believe and more.

"Sa mga narinig ko about you, I'm sure kayang-kaya mo 'yan," I found myself saying in encouragement. "Besides, alam mo naman, your kuya is always right. If he thinks you deserve that, it must be true."

That made her laugh. "I don't know. I'm just grateful he's always so supportive. He's like the best kuya ever." Then she bit her lip. "He's also very loyal. And smart. And charming. And honest. He'll always remember your birthday. And your anniversary... Just FYI."

I gave her a strange look when she kept going.

But Monica had an impish look on her face as if she already knew more than she was letting on.

Self-conscious, I cleared my throat and was relieved when Will came back to say that it was time to go to lunch.

He gestured his arm to direct Ninang Amy, Roger, and Monica motioning for them to go first.

Then I felt his hand on the small of my back.

Will's smile had an adorably diffident tinge to it when he met my gaze. "Tara?"

My tongue was stuck in my mouth. I merely jumped and went ahead.

Our ride to the buffet was the very quaint carabao-pulled *kalesa* ride. Given that, it was a very iconic yet very slow way to make the short distance across to the buffet area.

Monica had taken the bench seat beside me while Will sat up front with Ninang Amy and Roger holding up the rear.

Despite the heat, the weather was calm. Dark clouds loomed at the far end of the property as though it was going to rain at some point but not quite yet.

Naturally, Roger had more things to say about the humidity and the flies loitering about the pungent behind of the carabao.

But Monica was apparently very curious about everything about me for some reason, and shockingly, she already knew a lot.

"Kuya told me you're in a band."

I met Will's sideways glance, almost surprised, since I knew his opinion of my band was significantly less than favorable.

"Uh, maliit na band lang kami," I dismissed, self-effacingly. "In fact, nagsara yung bar sa BF kung saan kami usually nag-pe-perform."

"Oh, talaga? Sayang naman. I'm sure you're really good." Her frown indicated that she was as unhappy as I was about the fact despite having just met me. "Well, sana mag-open sila ulit or makahanap kayo ng ibang venue."

I could only nod and smile in appreciation—and amazement.

Based on all the stories from Catt and forgive my ignorant assumptions, I honestly thought Monica would be a spoiled bratty princess. On the contrary, she was gracious. She was thoughtful. She was kind. She was exactly as Ate Pilar had described.

Monica gushed on. "Still, that's all so exciting! I wish I was in a band. Kaya lang I'm already too busy with other activities."

I waved it away. "I'm sure mas marami kang talents. You'll have better things to aspire to." I blinked as I recalled one. "Like I heard from Tita that you're really good at cooking."

Monica's giggle was light and airy. "Ay, hindi naman. It's just a hobby." She grabbed my arm. "You should come to the house again though! I'd love to cook for you sometime."

I blinked again at her enthusiasm. "Oo ba," I replied with a shrug. "Basta hindi ko kailangan tumulong. Baka ma-ospital tayong lahat ng hindi oras."

Monica shot me an astonished look. "Sabi ni Kuya magaling ka daw magluto."

I shot the back of Will's head an even more astonished look. "Sinungaling!" I accused in a hoarse whisper.

That made Will chuckle low in his throat as he had obviously been eavesdropping and he turned, propping his arm across the back of the seat. "I meant 'okay lang'," he amended with a shrug. "Hindi naman ako na-lason last time, right?" He gave me a look and I tried not to laugh.

I almost had to shake my head to snap out of a daze. I almost felt like I was looking at a completely different person.

What the heck was going on??

28

Hello

The whole day went pretty much like that—light, easy-going, fun.

Will was just all kinds of surprising today.

Anything that anyone needed, he was more than happy to supply.

Even though he literally owned the place, he didn't demand any special treatment, didn't expect to be first in line for anything. He was entirely respectful of the staff. And it was obvious that they all thought highly of him in return.

Will was friendly, engaging, good-humored, and as I'd heard from several people already, not just Monica, he was definitely *maalaga*.

Plus, it was heartening to watch him interact with his sister. Their relationship seemed really fun, much like any normal family's, much like me and my own siblings. I didn't even know why I expected it to be any different.

Ninang Amy was also much impressed with Will's manners and candor and Roger definitely looked more comfortable conversing with the two siblings, not having to struggle with the language barrier.

Apparently, Roger enjoyed the novelty of eating on the banana leaves and drinking out of whole fresh coconuts. He thought the heritage museum was interesting if dusty and he had never stepped foot inside a Catholic church before. Churches looked different where he was from.

"Where are you guys based in Australia?"

"Melbourne."

Will's eyes lit up. "We lived in Melbourne for a few years when I was younger. My dad runs a business out of Perth and Sydney. But my favorite city has always been Melbourne."

"Me too!" Ninang Amy gave him a warm smile.

Will snapped his fingers a few times, trying to remember something. "There's this really great café, I forget the name. It's in an old brick building in the Upper West CBD. The food is great and the ambiance is just..."

But Roger was already nodding. "It already sounds good. Hey, if you're ever back in town, we should do a coffee."

Will looked surprised but pleased. "Oh, definitely, thank you."

Roger fished out a little card from inside his wallet. "Here's my card."

"And here's mine."

I was watching the exchange in slight disbelief and incredulity when Ninang Amy tugged on my arm—to ask the million-dollar question.

"Uy, Armi. Ba't ang bait ni Will? Akala ko ba suplado dapat 'yan?"

I wrinkled my nose since I couldn't come up with a rational answer to her question.

Given our first impressions of him, I had to do a mental rundown of his characteristics just to keep from feeling like I was going insane.

But they were still true. He still barely spoke unless spoken to. He was still wary of strangers. He still tended to be quite arrogant and self-assured. Only he didn't seem as offensive as he used to be.

As we sat at a table waiting for the cultural show in the Coconut Pavilion, Ninang Amy was busy admiring the décor and the wooden candelabra chandeliers. Monica and Roger were looking through some pictures on her camera, talking about apertures or something.

Will was standing nearby, talking to one of the property's hands presumably about the business that he was originally here to deal with.

I was preoccupied trying not to stare at him (sorry!) so I wasn't sure how this conversation came about but I overheard Ninang Amy ask Monica something.

"What about you, Monica?" she began, her eyes mischievous as she stirred the halo-halo in her plastic cup. "Wala ka pa ba'ng boyfriend? Siguradong marami kang manliligaw, right? Napaka-heartbreaker mo siguro."

Alarm bells rang in my head and as I expected, Monica stiffened. I looked over to meet Will's already anxious gaze as naturally, he had noticed too.

Ninang Amy went on in a hoarse whisper, winking, "Or if may secret boyfriend ka na, okay lang, hindi ko sasabihin sa kuya mo."

Monica looked even more flustered, her mouth gaping open.

I supposed it was an innocent question from Ninang Amy and some of my mother's own bloodline asserting itself, but knowing a little bit about Monica's history, especially regarding George, I knew it was a particularly sore topic.

I shot up to nudge Ninang Amy. "Ninang Amy, napaka-chismosa! I'm sure hindi kailangan ni Monica ng tulong mo mang-reto." I rolled my eyes and gestured to the stage. "The show is about to start and I'm really curious to see Roger's reaction to the *tinikling* dance," I proposed with a wide grin, giving Roger a brief look.

That made the two of them laugh and Ninang Amy began to describe our strange traditional dance to Roger.

I glanced over at Monica to check. Her cheeks were still red, her gaze on the floor but at least she looked relieved at the change of the subject.

Stepping back, I blew out a breath in relief myself. I happened to catch Will's grateful gaze and feeling self-conscious all over again, I quickly looked away. He was being so nice to us today. I just wanted to return the favor, especially where his wonderful sister was concerned.

Just as the show started, Monica spotted one of her school friends at another table and excused herself to go over to say hello.

I cast Ninang Amy and Roger another glance. Their heads were leaned towards each other, discussing the aspects of the show quietly as they watched. They seemed to really be enjoying themselves and I was glad that we'd had this opportunity.

I was about to turn to look for Will so that I could thank him properly when he came up beside me. I stilled for a moment, almost gasping in surprise, catching a light whiff of whatever that cologne was he was wearing.

Lord, bakit ang bango...?

He peered at my face, hesitating about something, always hesitating.

For some reason, I couldn't find the words to get started with to say thanks either.

I felt a light tap before Will rested his hand on my shoulder. His hand was warm and it was almost as though the heat from him crept up my neck and my face grew warm too.

"Armi..." he spoke low.

I swallowed hard before I dared to look up to his intense gaze. I had always tried never to be daunted by him. I wasn't about to start now. I pursed my lips, managing to raise my eyebrow to prompt, "Will?"

Will cracked another disarming grin and I could almost tell we were both in incredulous disbelief of the current situation.

My heart was pounding in my chest, in my ears, over the noise of the crowd and the performance in the pavilion. I couldn't stop staring at him but he didn't seem willing to look away either.

For a moment, it was like I almost didn't need to know or hear or say or do anything more. It was as though—

BEEP BEEP BEEP!

I jumped at my phone's text message alert tone which also

startled Will. He averted his gaze for a second to chuckle nervously, his hand still propped on my shoulder.

I shook my head to try to snap out of my daze, scrambling to get my phone out of my pocket to read the message.

The preview said it was from Ate Roweena and I swiped my phone unlocked. I was still on a bit of a high that I gasped in shock when I actually read the whole message, my eyebrows snapping together in bewilderment.

Will noticed and he leaned slightly closer, curious. "Is everything okay?"

I couldn't keep the shock out of my face even as I met his concerned gaze. I almost stammered, "Nasa presinto daw si Martin. Kasama si George."

Will's face blanked and he jerked his hand away as though touching me burned him.

"Naka-hit-and-run daw sila sa Antipolo at...may nahanap na drugs sa kotse."

My chest constricted and I almost started to heave.

Because I knew.

I knew this was the last straw.

The impropriety of my family in public, while an undesirable trait for any degree of social acceptance, was a triviality compared to if my brother went to jail for possession and manslaughter.

I almost thought I was going to collapse in distress and desolation but I was still staring up at Will.

The hollow expression on his face was all too readable.

"Nako." Ninang Amy stood up and made an abrupt motion to Roger to get going. "We need to go back. Siguradong kailangan ni Ate Adel ang tulong natin."

I blew out another breath, dropping my gaze. My mind was whirling and I was having difficulty collecting my bearings.

"You should leave now."

I looked up when Will spoke again and I noted his distant gaze.

My face hot, I swallowed hard again. My throat was sore from trying to hold back the urge to scream. I merely nodded in understanding, stepping back towards Ninang Amy and Roger who were hurrying us away.

The tour was over.

Everything was.

***

29

Kaso Kasi

"Armi."

"Armi!"

"Huy, Armi!"

I snapped back to the present, blinking at the bright lights in my face before meeting Boboy's pointed, irritated look.

I gazed out at the bar crowd who thankfully were still applauding as our band's set finished—even though the completely distracted bass player was still strumming. I quickly dropped my hands.

"Maraming salamat po!" Boboy raised his mic before doing an elaborate bow to the whoops and whistles of our audience.

I wiped my sweaty hands on my pants before unlatching my guitar strap from my neck. "Sorry, guys," I mumbled as I joined the others to pack up.

Shawi paused from organizing his drums to walk over and

thump hard on my back in consolation and understanding but he didn't say anything.

Frank Lloyd's gaze was across the bar to the counter where Boboy had headed over directly to talk with the establishment owner about possibly a permanent slot in their weekly performance line-up.

I grimaced upon seeing Boboy's shoulders slack in disappointment before the owner guy walked away.

More bad news.

Suffice it to say, none of us had been having a very happy New Year.

The whole of my Christmas had been blurred with conversations and apprehensions about talking to the police, having consultations with some lawyers, and making hospital visits to appease the injured old woman whom Martin and his friends had allegedly run over.

Ninang Amy and Roger had left weeks ago although most of their visit had been occupied with helping out with Martin's case.

And while she couldn't delay her return to Australia any longer, Ninang Amy had referred us to one of her Manila-based lawyer friends from college to help with handling everything.

It was a long road and it definitely wasn't over yet.

Shawi slid the door to the van outside shut once as we had loaded up all the equipment. "Ano daw sabi, p're?"

Boboy hopped into the driver's seat with a groan. "May house band na daw kasi sila so if ever hindi siya regular."

Frank Lloyd shrugged from the passenger seat. "Ayos na

rin," he reasoned. "At least may posibleng backup. Sa mga panahon ngayon hindi pwedeng isa lang ang diskarte."

"Medyo malayo nga lang," Shawi pointed out as he hopped into the back with me.

"Shawi, sa'yo na muna yung equipment ha," I told him. "Baka hindi nanaman ako makatakas sa trabaho next week."

"Diyan ka na ba permanently, Armi?" Frank Lloyd craned his neck to glance at me. "Akala ko balak mo umalis at some point?"

I merely shrugged. I was pretty sure I would get no end of complaints from my mother if I quit the one stable job I had, getting more and more necessary in helping my family out with the steady stream of money.

In another few weeks, I was supposed to be renegotiating my contract under Tito Boy's employment. I wished I had better options but I did not.

"Naku, hindi pwedeng hintayin mo lang ang kapalaran mo, 'tol. Kailangan kareerin 'yan," Shawi hooted.

You don't even know anything about business. You can barely keep a decent job.

I cringed at the other nagging voice in my head.

The one fortunate thing was that with everything so hectic, I'd been spared the embarrassment of having to face Will or anyone else any further. No doubt, they would be loath to associate with any one of us now anyway.

I stepped back onto the front stoop of my house after getting dropped off. I waved as Boboy's van drove away. "Salamat!"

I was dreading walking into the house because even though

it was so late, I already knew the sight and sounds that would greet me upon coming in.

My mom and dad, both looking worn and exhausted, sitting at the dining table going through the same paperwork, or having fallen asleep surrounded by it, having the same conversations and comments.

My mom would be moaning about the potential legal fees cleaning out what savings we had left. We were already in more debt than ever. Tito Boy would end up taking the house. And if the news got out, we'd be the laughingstock of the barangay.

"Basta lang huwag makulong si Martin. Drugs pa, sa lahat ng bagay," my dad would be pointing out again.

I shuffled quickly past them to go to my room. Ate Roweena was still at work, probably doing overtime for obvious reasons.

I sank in my bed and heaved a giant sigh, squeezing my eyes shut in frustration as if I could will the entire thing to go away.

Really, this was all my fault.

If I hadn't championed George to everyone else, he might not have had the influence over Martin and indeed all of us that he did. If I hadn't fallen for his sneaky charms, I would have been able to be more discerning with the truth about his claims.

I should have listened to Ate Roweena when she'd suggested that we disclose to everyone that George was a bad guy. That way perhaps I'd have been able to convince Martin to stop hanging out with him or at least my parents could have made him stop and all this would never have happened.

May mga tao talaga na hindi dapat pagkatiwalaan...
I blew out another breath, collapsing back onto my bed.
This was all my stupid fault.
And there was nothing I could do to fix it now.

The next day's chismis stream delivered by Stella only validated what we'd recently discovered.

"Bingka, takpan mo tenga mo," Mom barked abruptly as Stella came to the more salacious parts of her story.

Sprawled on the floor with her old iPad, Bingka jumped in surprise but she merely adjusted her headphones around her head and turned up the volume. She was only eleven but I was sure even she could feel the turmoil in the house.

I wanted to bang my head against the wall. Aside from gambling debts and suspicion of drug use, Stella didn't relay anything I didn't already know.

"Taga-Poveda?" my mom's eyes were as wide as I'd ever seen them as though she was about to faint.

Stella pursed her lips. "Sorry po, Tita. 'Yun lang ang narinig ko."

"Sinabi ko na nga ba," Mom huffed, sprawling back against the sofa, fanning herself with a folded up shopping catalogue booklet. "Hindi ko talaga nagustuhan 'yung batang 'yun. Masyadong pulido. Nakakaloko. Parang ang bait-bait, 'yun pala demonyo. Masamang impluwensiya sa kawawang anak ko."

I simply met Ate Roweena's tentative, knowing gaze.

For one thing, I was painfully aware that Mom was very

much "Team George" and had gone so far as to try to set George and I up on a date on more than one occasion. And for another, I was sure Martin wasn't exactly the innocent party Mom was imagining.

But I let my mom's comment slide. Clearly, she was distraught enough.

"Hay nako." Mom was still in hysterics as she got up from the couch. "Matawagan nga ang tatay n'yo. Sana naman maawa sa atin 'yung ale at hindi na palalain 'yung kaso."

Ate Roweena watched our mom depart before she herself slumped back onto the couch across from Stella and heaved a big sigh. "Kasalanan ko 'tong lahat," she claimed. "Dapat hindi ako nag-dalawang isip na sabihin kina Mommy ang totoo tungkol kay George."

My eyebrows snapped together in protest and I jumped to sit next to her. "Ano ka ba, Ate? Sa lahat ng tao, ikaw ang pinaka-walang kasalanan, 'no."

"True," Stella chimed in. "Lahat naman tayo naloko ni George eh. Huwag mo na siyang pag-aksayahan ng oras isipin."

"Oo nga, Ate. Tignan mo," I coaxed. "Mga tatlong oras ng K-drama, I'm sure gagaan din ang loob natin. Diba 'no, Stella?" I prompted with a grin, reaching for the TV remote. "Anong gusto n'yong panoorin today?"

Stella looked uneasy in her seat as she gestured backwards. "Um, actually, kailangan ko na'ng umalis."

I sat up. "Ha? Kararating mo lang, a."

She made a face. "Ah, medyo tinotopak kasi si Nick eh. Sabi niya hindi na raw ako dapat magpunta dito ulit."

My jaw dropped in incredulity. "What the F? Kaya ba nag-aantay lang siya sa kotse as labas?" I clenched my fists. "Sasapakin ko 'yang Nick na 'yan eh."

Stella shrugged. "Saka na-mention pala pati ni Nick kay Tita ang nangyari. Pasaway daw si Martin kasi wala daw class at disiplina ang pamilya n'yo. Supposedly, hindi na daw tayo pwede maging friends."

I groaned. I seriously wanted to beat up that pompous *sumbungero* jerk.

But Stella dismissed the issue with a wave. "Hayaan mo 'yun. I'm sure ma-ge-get over din ni Nick 'yang mood na 'yan." She stood up to head off. "In the meantime, kitakits na muna. At good luck kay Martin."

"Salamat, dude." I stood up to give her a grateful pat on the shoulder.

"Sige, Weena. Bye, Armi," Stella bid before leaving.

But I made a point to peer over our gate to try to catch Nick's gaze to give him the darkest glare I could muster. *Lagot ka sa'kin sa susunod, Nicolas.* And I didn't stop glaring at him until Stella had hopped into the car and driven away.

I blew out an exaggerated exasperated breath as I turned back into the living room. "Haaay. Kailangan pa talaga'ng idamay ang banal niya'ng Tita," I hissed my complaint with a shake of my head. "Tsk. Siguradong sira na talaga ang impression sa'tin nila Lance. Paano ba 'yan?"

Ate Roweena's forehead creased in surprise at the sudden mention of his name. "Ni Lance?" she echoed in soft mocking. "Nako Armi, matagal ko nang na-let go ang posibilidad na 'yon. Asa pa tayo."

I met her gaze in desolate disquiet. She was probably right.
We no longer had a choice but to let those possibilities go.
All of them.
All of them.
Asa pa tayo.

30

Maligayang Bati

"Shh—shh!" I tried to shush Bingka as we crept into the room but she was so excited, she couldn't help giggling—which, in turn, was making me laugh.

I sneaked a peek at Ate Roweena to make sure she was still asleep and I almost tripped on the edge of a blanket spilling off my unmade bed.

That set Bingka off again and the noise finally woke up Ate Roweena.

"Mmm, anong ginagawa n'yo diyan?" Ate Roweena moaned in complaint, squinting at the bright morning sun in her half-open eyes.

"SURPRISE!"

Bingka jumped onto Ate Roweena's bed.

"ARAY—!"

I laughed again before producing the wrapped-up little present I'd been keeping behind my back, sitting at the edge of the bed and holding it out to her. "Alam ko next weekend pa dapat pero happy birthday, Ate!"

"Happy birthday, Ate!" Bingka echoed happily. "Gising na, Ate!"

Ate Roweena sat up, looking astonished but smiling. "Ha? Kayo talaga." She took the gift and put it on her lap. "Ano ba 'yan?" She rubbed her face. "Ni hindi n'yo man lang muna ako pinag-hilamos."

Bingka giggled away again. "Buksan mo na 'yung gift, Ate, dali, dali!"

Ate Roweena chuckled at her excitement and tore into the little box but she stopped short, her eyes wide upon seeing what was inside, and didn't finish unwrapping it. "Hala." She met my gaze. "Armi."

I rolled my eyes and snatched the wrapper away from her to leave just the box of the brand new, shiny, latest model iPhone.

"Okay ba, Ate? Maganda po ba? Ang ganda 'no?" Bingka prompted, bouncing on the bed. "Galing sa'min ni Ate Armi 'yan. Nag-ipon po kami buong taon. Meron pa nga'ng sukli sa alkansya ko, eh." Her face was full of pride.

Ate Roweena put her hand on my arm and just gave me that look but I already knew what she was thinking.

With everything that was going on, she would have us all believe her needs should be everyone's last priority. But that was Ate Roweena. Selfless to a fault. It always had been.

I dismissed her concerns with a wave. I'd already been saving that money up for a long time. It would have barely made a dent in whatever debt we were in anyway, and I believed that despite everything, or perhaps *because* of everything, of all people, Ate Roweena still deserved to have a great birthday.

"Ate, seriously, kailangan mo na'ng palitan 'yung lumang phone mo. Grabe na ha. Ibang level."

She took a deep breath, only speaking after a pause, her tone awed, grateful. "Maraming salamat."

I gave her a small smile then made a face again. "Well, anyway, last na 'yan. Obviously, mamumulubi na tayo this year. Diba 'no, Bingka?" I nudged her.

Bingka grinned. "Don't worry, mga Ate. Kung makulong si Kuya eh di baka sa wakas magkaka-sarili na tayong kwarto!"

Ate Roweena almost choked on her sudden laughter.

I shot Bingka a look of disbelief, reaching out to whack the back of her head. "Ikaw talaga'ng bata ka. Pasaway ka rin, ano?"

And the three of us burst out laughing.

"Bingka, kunin mo nga si Basti," Ate Roweena called from the kitchen.

The little dog was barking like mad trying to chase the end bit of the Christmas lights that my dad and I were only just finally taking down off the roof.

I was holding the ladder steady for Dad, trying to shoo Basti away.

My mom passed through the living room holding a big plastic basket of laundry and paused to give us a critical look. "Iwan na lang kaya natin 'yang ilaw," she began after a moment of thought. "Ilang buwan na din nakakabit."

Dad gave her a flat look. "Gusto mo ba iwan na lang natin nakakabit 'yung ilaw?"

I rolled my eyes again at their usual exchange.

"Lagyan din po natin ng decorations para sa birthday party ni Ate next weekend," Bingka suggested with an innocent grin as she coaxed Basti towards the couch.

"Ay, Bingka," Ate Roweena started, turning slightly from her cooking. "Hindi ko naman kailangan ng party. Matanda na ako."

Bingka looked confused. "Walang party?"

I supposed I could understand why it wouldn't make sense to a child.

"Tayu-tayo lang next weekend, Bingka," Ate Roweena met my mother's gaze for a brief moment. "Pero bibili ako ng cake. Huwag ka'ng mag-alala."

"Armi," Mom started even as she headed out the back door. "Parang nakita ko naiwan naka-on 'yung electric fan sa kwarto n'yo kanina. Walang tao. Sayang kuryente. Kailangan mas maingat tayo ngayon, ha?"

"Opo, Mommy."

"Alam n'yo po ba 'yung birthday party daw ni Francesca, pupunta kami'ng lahat sa Sta. Rosa tapos manlilibre siya ng Enchanted Kingdom!" Bingka announced, her eyes already wide in excitement even as she petted the dog beside her.

"Sinong Francesca 'yan?" Dad spoke up with a frown. "Hindi natin kilala 'yan. Hindi ka pwede pumunta."

Bingka's jaw dropped in shock and dismay.

"Daddy, best friend siya ni Bingka," I reminded him. "Remember? Ilang taon na sila'ng magkaibigan. Naka-bisita na nga dito sa'tin 'yung mga magulang niya, eh."

Dad merely narrowed his eyes, immediately yielding. "Ah, o sige." He shot me a look. "Armi, ikaw na bahala, ha. Siguraduhin mo'ng matino ang mga 'kaibigan' na 'yan. Baka pati si Bingka magaya pa kay Martin. Mahirap na."

I glanced up and met the expectant, already worried gaze of Ate Roweena.

Even our dad blamed himself for what had happened to Martin. I also knew he was even a bit embarrassed because he fully recalled I had tried to warn him that night. But even with all that, Dad didn't seem to know how to compensate except to overreact to the situation. At his age, I supposed all he wanted to worry about was providing for his family and not these sorts of things.

I gave him a gentle reassuring look. "Don't worry, Daddy. Ako na po ang bahala."

The doorbell rang and Basti scrambled away from Bingka to run outside.

The gate clunked open before I could even turn to see that it was Martin coming in with Ninang Amy's lawyer friend.

"Good afternoon, po!" Lynette called out with a smile.

"Uyy, Basti!" Martin caught the dog as it ran up to him.

Dad dusted off his hands and came down the ladder with a sigh. "O, Lynette. Kamusta na?" His forehead had creased automatically, obviously not under any assumption that the two were bringing good news.

But Lynette's smile widened. "Good news, po."

By the time Mom had been called inside to sit down with Lynette and Martin, I'd already overheard the headlines.

They had managed to agree to a settlement out of court with the hit and run for reckless imprudence resulting to injury. And although the possession case was still underway, it was successfully argued that there was insufficient evidence linking Martin to it.

"Ay, salamat sa Diyos!" Mom cried out, fanning her face with her hand before turning to clutch at Ate Roweena's hand.

Dad slumped back against the chair, incredible relief visible on his worn face before he finally looked over at Martin's sheepish expression. Dad leaned over to pound on his shoulder. "Ayos, anak."

Bingka and I were sitting on the couch and I turned to give her a triumphant high-five but with a teasing shrug. "Sorry, Bingka. I guess hindi tayo magkaka-sariling kwarto."

Bingka gave me a cheeky grin. "Baka next time."

I almost shouted out my laughter but I just gave her an incredulous look with a shake of my head.

"So..." Dad shifted in his chair to regard Lynette with a look. "Ano na lang ang kulang?" His face wrinkled again as he steeled himself to discuss the money terms.

Lynette shook her head. "Ayos na po lahat, Tito. Enough na po 'yung nabayad so far."

Mom quirked her head in surprise. "Ha?" She met Dad's gaze in curiosity. "Paano nangyari 'yun?"

"Inasikaso na po ni Amy 'yung natira."

My parents' eyes nearly popped out of their heads.

So did mine, actually, as I was sneakily fully aware how much the entire thing actually cost—there was the hospital bill, the lawyer consultations, the fiscal office's "fees." If I had to make a guess, I would say that we'd only paid about ten percent of the full amount so far.

Lynette had said her congratulations and goodbyes and left through the gate before Dad turned to Mom, his expression one of protest and indignation.

"Adel, binayaran lahat ni Amy? Ang laking halaga nu'n. Paano natin ibabalik 'yang utang? Ano na?"

Mom took a moment to think about it then made a face to dismiss him. "Naku, laking pasalamat natin kina Amy and Roger. Sila naman ang mayaman!" she exclaimed. "Mas mabuti na't sila magbayad," she added with the most inappropriate of smug huffs.

"Mommy!" Ate Roweena hissed in scolding.

I shook my head in disbelief.

Granted, my mom had just been through a severe ordeal but I guessed it was too much to hope that she should have learned something.

"Huwag kayong mag-alala." Mom clasped her hands with a gleeful smile. "Ipagdadasal natin sila bukas pagkatapos ng misa. Mag-aalay din tayo kay Santo Niño. Pati kandila na rin." She fussed about the living room, touching several religious statuettes in reverence.

Dad merely grunted at his wife's whimsy, likely so used to it after all these years it no longer fazed him. He turned to Martin with a stern look. "Ikaw Martin, tama na 'yang pakik-isama sa mga kaibigan mo'ng masamang impluwensiya, ha?"

Martin still looked fully embarrassed. "Don't worry, Dad. Uuwi daw si George sa probinya pagkatapos nito. Na-assign siya sa Davao for work so hindi n'yo na po kailangan alala-hanin 'yon."

I breathed a huge sigh of relief. "Gosh, mabuti naman," I couldn't help a mumble.

I only hoped Martin had learned *his* lesson and would not seek to associate with anyone else of a similar deceptive nature in the future.

I was sure all of us had simultaneously felt the same heavy burden having been lifted from our shoulders.

The case was over. Our family's reputation had miraculously been spared. It would be as though nothing even happened. Everything could go back to normal.

Ate Roweena patted my back, a serene smile back on her face as she studied the frown still on my face. "May problema pa ba?"

I pursed my lips, slightly annoyed at what was running through my head at the moment. "Ah, wala naman. Mabuti lang at hindi kumalat sa barangay 'yung balita bago na-resolve." I shook my head and sighed again. "Sana hindi lang rin nalaman ni Will. Nakakahiya talaga."

"Armi, I'm sure mas maraming importanteng iniisip ang Will Salcedo na 'yan," she reassured me. "At hindi ko naman ma-imagine na may ilalala pa lalo ang tingin niya sa'tin, right?"

I blinked, fully taken aback.

Aray ko naman.

Ate Roweena for the painful truth.

31

Pagbalik

Come mid-week there was even more good news.

As soon as Martin had gone back to school, he finally decided what he wanted to finish college with: a pre-law degree. And given how many shifts he'd done already, he only needed to complete a few more units in order to graduate.

I had to hand it to my dad after all as it was just as he had said. The whole debacle with Martin's case had miraculously wised him up.

With everything to be thankful for, things were more upbeat in the house by the time Ate Roweena's birthday weekend rolled around.

"Oist! Pwede pagamitin n'yo naman 'yung bagong phone sa may-ari minsan," I told off Martin and Bingka who were both on the couch, fussing over the shiny new gadget.

Ate Roweena merely laughed from the kitchen as she stirred some noodles in the big wok. "Okay lang naman.

Although sabi ko na nga ba ako lang din ang magluluto ng sarili kong handa para sa birthday ko eh. Wala ba talaga'ng tutulong sa inyo?"

I laughed, pushing up off the couch to approach the kitchen. "Sige na nga. Ano pa ba'ng kulang for tonight?" I asked, surveying the kitchen table behind my sister where a few modest dishes were sitting in some pots and trays.

"Paki-takpan na muna 'yung *bandehado* ng foil para hindi langawin. May Tupperware pa sa cabinet kung kailangan mo. Patapos ko na rin lutuin 'tong palabok," Ate Roweena replied, gesturing to the wok.

"Uy, favorite ko 'yan, Ate!" Bingka exclaimed. "Pwede po gawa ka din para sa graduation party ko?"

"Pano, Bingka?" Martin chimed in even as he held the phone at his arm's length to take a selfie of the two of them. "Sabay pa pala tayo'ng ga-graduate this year, eh."

"Oo nga 'no! Gujab talaga si Kuya!" Bingka grinned wide, posing, holding up Korean heart fingers as the phone camera clicked.

"Saka kailangan din pala dumaan sa Goldilocks para bilhin 'yung cake mamaya," Ate Roweena added.

"Sasabihan ko si Daddy. Good mood na 'yon this week," I told her with a wink.

There was a loud clanging at the gate and I hurried towards the window to check to see who it was.

"Magandang tanghali, mga kapitbahay!" Mrs. Casal yelled out from behind the metal bars of our gate. She seemed satisfied to stay on that side of the gate even as she primed the atmosphere for incoming *chismis*.

Mom emerged from the backyard, coming around the side

of the house, wiping her slightly bubbly hands on her apron. "O, Chicha, kamusta na?"

"Nakita n'yo ba? Siguro naman nakita n'yo na, ano?" Mrs. Casal's eager grin was accentuated by her bright red lipstick and smoky eye shadow.

"Nakita ang alin?" Mom prompted, looking puzzled.

"May tao daw ulit sa bahay sa tapat," Mrs. Casal announced. "Mukhang bumalik na yata 'yung mga Ortega."

Her voice was quite loud it carried well into the house and when I glanced back towards the kitchen, I wasn't surprised to meet Ate Roweena's already wary gaze.

"Ay, hindi ko pa alam 'yan, mare! Ano daw?" Mom leaned against the gate, just as eager to hear more about it as Mrs. Casal was to share.

"May mga nakita daw na dumaan na kotse kanina. Ang gagarbo daw. 'Yung isa kulay gold."

My eyes lit up. *Kotse ni Will?*

The car talk seemed to interest Martin and he stood up to go outside, leaving Bingka on the couch to play with the phone.

I took that as a cue to go outside too. Normally, I wouldn't be interested in Mrs. Casal's usual offering of gossip but obviously, this was different.

"Baka naman chismis lang 'yan, mare, ha," Mom began. "Paano ka naman nakaka-siguro?"

"Ay, tinawagan daw nila ulit si Rosa para tumulong sa pag-linis ng bahay. M-W-F daw," Mrs. Casal relayed with authority.

By this time, Ate Roweena had come out of the house

as well, just in time to see a delivery truck labeled 'Landers' rumble down the avenue and turn down the street.

Ate Roweena, Martin, Mom, and I all peered over the top of our gate to stare in expectation at the compound across the street where this person was jogging across to the end of the closed-again-until-today, huge, rust-colored metal gate where he clasped at the handle to pull it back, seeming in slow-motion.

I could've sworn I almost heard the ominous music from "2001: A Space Odyssey" as the gate swung open which must indeed indicate the return of the house's occupants.

My mom squealed in delight. "Naku, Rowena! Bumalik na si Lance!" She tapped Ate Roweena's arm excitedly but she caught herself before she could start clapping. "Ay, sandali lang." She made a face. "Galit nga pala tayo dapat sa kanila."

"Mommy," Ate Roweena began calmly. "Hayaan n'yo na 'yung tao. Hindi ba sila pwedeng umuwi sa sarili nilang bahay nang hindi natin sila pinag-chi-chismisan?"

Mrs. Casal regarded Ate Roweena's face in good humor before meeting my mom's gaze again. "Well," she began. "Good luck sa inyong lahat." She raised her hand in a wave. "Sige at ibabalita ko rin kay Dolor 'to."

Mom's eyes narrowed as she watched her friend walk away. "Aba, ano ba'ng akala ni Chicha? May pa-'good luck' pa siya."

Martin quipped with a smirk, "Alam naman kasi ng buong barangay na nag-split sila Ate at Lance eh. Last chance na 'to ni Inday—ARAY!"

I whacked the back of his head to shush him but he just snickered.

Mom huffed. "At sino ba'ng nagsabi'ng tatanggapin natin ulit si Lance ngayon?" she declared haughtily. "Matapos ang perwisyo'ng dinala niya? Hmph." She turned to go back to the house, beckoning Martin over. "Martin, hanapin mo nga 'yung tatay mo. Kailangan masabi ko sa kanya ang balita."

Once our mom and Martin were out of earshot, I leaned back against our gate to regard Ate Roweena with a tentative look.

"Okay ka lang, Ate?"

Ate Roweena fidgeted in her stance, only now displaying some level of anxiety. "Nako, Armi, baka kung anu-ano na nga ang pinagsasabi ng mga kapitbahay natin. Huwag naman sana."

I wrinkled my nose. "Hayaan mo sila. Inggit lang mga 'yun."

Knowing what I knew about Lance, I had to confess I was a little bit excited for my sister. If I was going to be an optimist, I could totally interpret Lance's return as partly with the intention of being close to her again.

Besides, I was also a hundred percent sure that Ate Roweena still had feelings for Lance too. I could already foresee a happy ending in their future. Fingers crossed.

"Bakit ba kasi kailangan pa niya'ng bumalik?" Ate Roweena distressed as we both walked back inside. "Basta Armi, ha," she began to me with a determined tone. "Kalimutan na natin si Lance. Kunyari walang nangyari."

I bit back my grin. "Oo ba. Sinabi mo eh," I replied, a mischievous catch in my tone as I met her gaze again.

She blushed and pushed me away. "Shut up."

"Yihee!"

Ate Roweena rolled her eyes with her groan, "Armi, ano ka ba? Tigilan mo nga 'yan!"

But I just kept laughing as we headed back inside.

32

Mundo

"Isa pa?" Dad asked Bingka at the dining table. "Uubusin mo ba 'tong buong cake, anak?" He sounded reprimanding but his expression looked more amused than anything.

Bingka beamed up at him. "Opo, please!"

Dad chuckled in resignation, reaching for the knife to cut another piece from what was left of Ate Roweena's birthday cake. "Sige na nga, pero hati tayo ha?"

Bingka bobbed her head in agreement and enthusiasm before she glanced backwards. "Ate, mali nanaman po 'yung spelling ng pangalan mo, o." She was pointing to the 'Happy birthday' inscription on the cake, the name notably missing an 'e'.

Ate Roweena was sitting on the couch in the living room showing Mom something on her new phone while Basti slept by her feet. "Okay lang 'yan," she said with a smile and a shrug. "Kung gusto mo, unahin n'yo kainin 'yung part na 'yun."

Dad was already carefully slicing the cake. "Ayan, tanungin mo ulit sa nanay mo kung bakit kasi kailangan kakaiba ang spelling ng pangalan mo."

"Baka po may typo sa birth certificate ni Ate," Bingka guessed, leaning over the table.

"Typo? Aba, parang wala pa'ng computer nung mga panahon na 'yon, anak. Maliban na lang kung may typo 'yung kamay ng nanay n'yo," Dad suggested with a wry tone and Bingka laughed again.

But Mom was looking quite intrigued by Ate Roweena's phone, her head bent over the little gadget and not paying attention to the conversation. "Hala, Rowena, kunin mo nga ito, o. 'iPhone is disabled' daw—naku!" She shoved the phone back to my sister, presumably having done something wrong with it.

Ate Roweena didn't look disturbed at all. She merely took the phone back to wait the five minutes, shaking her head in bemusement. Then she called out to me, "Armi, sigurado ka'ng hindi mo kailangan ng tulong?"

Elbow-deep in dishwashing suds at the kitchen sink, I looked over my shoulder. "Oo naman," I assured with a wink. "Relax ka lang diyan, birthday girl."

Martin burst into the house just then, prompting Mom to get up and start. "Hoy Martin, tulungan mo nga ang Ate mo sa kusina."

"Yes, Mommy." He flashed her a charming grin before coming to sidle up beside me, grabbing a towel to clear the dish rack.

I shot him a sideways curious look as he seemed a bit breathless. "O, saan ka galing?"

"Sa park."

"Sa park?" I echoed in mocking. "At ano nanamang kaloko-han ang ginagawa mo sa park ng ganitong oras?"

Martin tsked. "Ate talaga. Don't you trust me anymore?"

I narrowed my eyes at him. "Trust me ka d'yan. Ikaw Martin ha," I reprimanded, already having to make an effort not to jump to conclusions. "Huwag ka na'ng magpapa-sangkot sa mga gawain ni George. Lahat tayo naloko n'yan."

"Ooh, ibang level ang bitterness," he teased.

I grimaced at his levity. "Hoy, pasalamat ka't sinwerte ka this time. Ang mga pagkakataon na ganyan, hindi nauulit."

Martin rolled his eyes as he sighed. "Hay nako, Ate. Minsan daig mo pa si Will Salcedo sa kasungitan. Cut all ties with George daw..." he muttered, almost to himself. "'*Don't waste your chance for a good future*,'" he mocked a deeper hollow voice with his impression of Will.

I snorted in fully incredulous disbelief. "Ha? At kailan naman sinabi ni Will Salcedo 'yan sa'yo?"

"Last week sa piskal."

My heart stopped. "Ano?"

"Ay, shet!" He slapped his forehead with his palm. "Secret nga pala dapat 'yon! Uy, wag mo'ng sabihin kina Mommy, ha?" he implored, giving me a wide-eyed look. "Sabi ni Will, 'wag ko daw sabihin kahit kanino."

My eyes were so wide in shock as well, I couldn't even blink. "K-Kasama n'yo si Will sa fiscal's office? Si Will Salcedo?"

"Oo na nga!" He repeated irritably before continuing to mumble to himself. "Sinabihan pa man din ako ni Tita Amy na makinig sa kanya. Shut up ka na, Martin! Hay naku, ang sama pati ng tingin sa'kin nu'ng mayabang na 'yun—"

I was already striding to the hallway, my dripping hands struggling to urgently compose my scandalized question to Ninang Amy on my phone messenger app.

I paused for a split second to check the time. Melbourne was a few hours ahead of Manila but I figured Ninang Amy would still be awake—*better still* be awake. I needed answers!

I absolutely *could not* believe that Will would have willingly involved himself in these dealings with Martin and George for things that were clearly George's own fault. It made zero sense.

I watched the messenger screen on my phone intently, waiting for the three dots to move and after the longest two minutes ever, I almost jumped, my eyes widening as I read Ninang Amy's replies.

Akala ko talaga alam mo.

Si Will ang nag-asikaso ng lahat.

Abugado. Ospital. Lahat. Kulang na nga lang awayin n'ya ako eh. Kailangan daw siya ang magbayad kasi siya ang may kasalanan.

Kung hindi daw siya napangunahan ng pag-mamataas, nasabi daw sana niya kaagad yung tungkol kay George, at baka naiwasan yung nangyari kay Martin.

Hindi mo nga talaga alam??

I looked up from reading, still bewildered at the ridiculously ridiculous surprising turn of events. *What the F?* I furrowed my eyebrows in the struggle of trying to figure out what it all meant.

I could imagine Will would have hated every minute.

There was no way he could have even avoided speaking to George or at the very least he'd had to have tolerated his presence in order to get everything resolved. And then to pay for everything!

My stomach churned with remorse at how horrible I had always been to Will since the first time I'd met him and all the unfair criticism that I had encouraged his way.

I groaned in frustration, slumping against the wall. *Oh my god, Armi. Ang bitch mo nga talaga!*

Ate Roweena found me stalled in the hallway, holding my phone, a blank stare on my face. She gave me a strange look as she passed by. "O, Armi, okay ka lang?"

I straightened up, clearing my throat. "Ah...oo." I took a deep breath to try to clear my head and my gaze dropped to my hands. "Ay, shet." I followed Ate Roweena back out to the kitchen so I could finish wiping my hands and my now-wet phone.

Ate Roweena had gone back to the couch to sit with Mom again, the iPhone having been re-enabled. Dad and Bingka were bringing the last of the cake plates to Martin at the sink.

As I crossed the living room, I cocked my head. "Ano 'yun?"

"Ha?" Ate Roweena looked up at me.

I thought I heard what sounded like an electric guitar.

Basti jerked up and began barking.

Mom sat up on the couch, her eyebrows furrowed too. "Anong ingay 'yon?" she asked, so I was assured I wasn't just imagining things.

Bingka skipped to the window. "Parang may tumutugtog galing sa labas."

"Pebrero na, a," Dad remarked. "May nangangaroling pa ba n'yan?"

I blinked, straining to hear. I could tell it was definitely an electric guitar playing. And whatever it was sounded distinctly like the leading strains of a 'IV of Escapades' song.

I was closest to the door and I pushed outside to check it out, stopping short in an instant.

My eyes widened in stunned shock when I peeked over our wall and saw my band set up on the street in front of our house. "What the heeeeell?"

The guys had borrowed extension cords to plug the amps and stuff through our gate and into our house. I hadn't even noticed.

The rest of my family arrived following me, all gawking at the scene unfolding before us.

Except for Martin who stood grinning beside me and I guessed he must have been the one who had helped them set up—earlier, at the park.

There was Frank Lloyd on lead guitars, Shawi on the drums, Jen on bass, and Boboy with the microphone.

And then there was Lance. He was holding a giant bouquet of two dozen pink roses. His gaze was pinned on Ate Roweena with the most earnest of expressions as he stood beside Boboy in the middle who was crooning out the lyrics.

Aking sinta. . .

Ate Roweena's jaw had dropped in surprise and pleasure. She moved to unlatch the gate and swung it open to step outside while the rest of the family hurriedly filed out after her.

I almost choked in happiness for my sister and my heart raced in excitement and delight.

Having a band finally paid off.

Take that, everyone.

I leaned against the half-open gate in leisure, even as I glanced sideways to make sure to keep my mom and dad or Bingka or Basti from interrupting the performance. The dazed expression on my sister's face was priceless. I didn't want anything to interrupt her moment.

I almost didn't notice the other person standing back in the shadows across the street.

My heart skipped a beat when I met his gaze.

Will.

But he didn't move. He didn't come over. His intense gaze just held mine steadily. My expression neutralized and I relaxed but didn't move from my own stance either. The two of us simply let the soothing music and the sweet promise of the song fill the air.

This time was for Ate Roweena and Lance.

The *harana* was starting to draw a crowd on our street —neighbors having finished their evening meals, some still even holding plates or glasses of drinks for washing, yet some looked like they had already been in bed and been woken up from the noise.

When the song moved into its second chorus, Jen stepped away from the group, still holding her guitar, and I realized she was walking towards me.

Before I knew what was going on, she had slid the strap of the guitar over my shoulder to prop the instrument in my hands.

My eyes widened in surprise but Jen just winked at me and nudged me towards the others. I glanced over at Ate

Roweena with a grin before I quickly hopped up to take my spot just beside Shawi, easily picking up the bass line.

Jen pulled out her cellphone to step back and take a video of all of us just as the song was about to go into the bridge.

By the time the song went into instrumental, the crowd around us was singing along, taking videos and pictures of our impromptu concert, and howling at the lovestruck couple in the center of the scene who was simply staring at each other in adoring anticipation.

My grin widened as we all played the hell out of the song. We weren't called "Anywhere/Anytime" for nothing and it was probably our best performance ever.

Frank Lloyd was going to town on his guitar solo. Shawi looked like he was concentrating for once. Boboy "The Showman" was dancing around until he picked back up on the chorus again. And with the closing strains of the coda fading, everyone erupted in cheers.

The cheering got even louder when Lance stepped up closer to hand Ate Roweena the flowers which she received with a shy but happy smile.

I turned to Boboy to give him a high-five. "Yes!"

Boboy grinned back at me and went to give the rest of the guys high-fives too.

I whirled around to look for Will but the thick crowd was also dispersing and several people were blocking the way to stop to take selfies around the band setup.

I craned my neck around, searching for what felt like too many minutes, but the moment I clapped eyes on him—he was still standing across the street, past the chaos of other barangay people—someone tugged my arm back.

Martin was discreetly trying to point at something, whispering hoarsely by my ear, "Uy Ate, si Will Salcedo ba 'yun? Ano naman kaya ang ginagawa niya dito?"

I pursed my lips, getting confused all over again, my brain repeating Martin's question. What *was* Will doing here? He didn't look like he was even going to come over and say hello.

I shook my head to clear it again, to rationalize.

Of course not. Why would he come over?

He was probably just here for Lance, having changed his mind and given his stamp of approval for Lance's pursuit of my sister after all. And everything he'd done for Martin was only to appease his guilty conscience about George, like he'd told Ninang Amy.

Those had to be the only reasons. Right?

An inkling of a thought, of another different potential reason, was nagging in the back of my mind. I told it to shut up.

But Mom was making a face. "Susmaryosep, kasama pa rin ba ni Lance 'yang supladong 'yan?" she lamented in distaste. "Baka as usual, nag-mamayabang at binabantayan ang kaibigan niya."

OMG. My stomach churned in annoyance and remorse.

My mom didn't even know that we probably owed Will, what with how he had handled and paid for everything that Martin and yes, the entire family, had just gone through.

Mom squealed in excitement first. "Naku! Kung hindi ko lang paborito si Lance eh hindi ko rin papansinin 'yan. Maski mayaman siya. Sa susunod, sasabihin ko sa tatay n'yo iiwasan natin 'yang Will Salcedo na 'yan."

I frowned. It was really hard to hear. I wanted to shout and correct her but my tongue felt stuck to the roof of my mouth.

Besides, Will hadn't wanted any credit. He wasn't interested in recognition. For him, it was the principle of the thing. Even though we could never pay him back.

My chest felt heavy at the thought.

We could never, ever pay him back.

And when I looked up again, Will was gone.

***

33

Viral

Laughter pealed through the house when I arrived at Boboy's one evening the next week. Pushing in through the front door, I found Jen and Stella at the dining table where Jen's laptop had been set up.

I plunked my bag on the couch, already casting the laughing pair a strange look as I approached. "Ano nanaman ang pinagtatawanan n'yo d'yan?"

Stella whirled around. "O Armi, ba't ngayon ka lang?"

"Ay, umalis na sila Kuya," Jen told me. "Hindi daw sila sigurado kung dadating ka or what."

I rolled my eyes. "Gosh. Don't they trust me anymore?" I mocked an imitation of Martin and shook my head.

"Saan ka nga ba galing?" Stella gave me a suspicious look.

I gave her a pointed look right back. "At bakit? Sinabi ba ni Nick friends na tayo ulit?"

Stella just laughed. "Pagbigyan mo na 'yang asawa ko. Alam mo naman 'yon."

"Hay nako, alam ko talaga," I could only agree, putting my hand up to receive her high-five.

"Teka na, Ate Armi." Jen tugged on my arm to gesture my attention towards her screen. "Look, o. Lampas 4,000 views na 'yung harana video natin!"

My nearly eyes popped out. "Ha?"

"Pinost ko siya para sa YouTube channel launch ng 'Anywhere/Anytime'," she explained.

I was still in shock over the numbers as I propped my hands on Jen's chair to gawk at her screen over her shoulder. "What? Hindi nga!"

"Dude, hashtag harana is trending." Stella winked even as the muted strains of our performance streamed from the tinny laptop speaker as Jen played the video again.

I had to close my mouth, my jaw having dropped.

Jen squealed as she gazed at the screen herself. "Yesss! They lived happily ever after talaga! Sabi ko na nga ba bet ko sila Ate Roweena at Kuya Lance eh. Perfect couple!"

Stella was shaking Jen's shoulder in excitement that could not be held back either. "Oh my god, napaka-sweet!" she cooed. "Sana nandun ako sa inyo last week, Armi."

Having gotten over my initial shock, I smiled as I watched the feed. "Sobrang bagay talaga sila, 'no?"

"Hala, nako, actually," Stella couldn't help but remark. "Masyado silang dalawa'ng mabait. Good luck talaga sa kanila."

I stuck my tongue out at her. "Ikaw talaga. Palibhasa under mo si Nick."

"Eh, ikaw Ate Armi? Nasaan ang happily ever after mo?" Jen asked, her expression already mischievous.

I rolled my eyes again. "Pliz. Asa pa," I replied. "'Wag mo nga kami i-compare. Mga anghel lang like Ate Roweena at mga demonyita like Stella get happy endings."

Stella made a grotesque face at me before pointing out, "Ayaaan, ang lakas kasi manabla."

"Ikaw na lang next, Jen, ha." I patted her shoulder in encouragement as the video ended with the crazy howling and clapping again.

"Hah. I'm too busy working on my career," Jen huffed with a pretend snobbish look. "At mukhang magiging busy tayo anyway. Tuwang-tuwa si Kuya Boboy. Kailangan na daw i-organize 'yung MTV taping natin. At saka may mga nagpapa-book pati ng harana gigs," she went on. "Tamang-tama for Valentine's!"

My jaw dropped in pleasure again. "Yeees...ayos 'yan!" I gave Jen a high-five too.

"Aba, okay na side business 'yan, a," Stella elbowed me.

"Mag-set-setup pa nga daw ng bagong cellphone si Kuya at gusto nila sana mag-pa-studio group pic ng banda nung Sunday pero wala kasi ulit si Ate Armi." Jen gave me a questioning look. "Nasaan ka ba last Sunday? At nasaan ka nga kanina? Hindi ka daw sumasagot ng phone."

I had to pause for a second. "Nasa work shempre," I fibbed. "Saan pa ba ako pupunta?"

Stella gave me a narrow-eyed look. She knew me well enough to know when I wasn't telling the truth. But she simply changed the subject by pointing to the screen again. "Ang ganda ng banner ha, Jen."

"Ay, thank you!" Jen beamed in appreciation. "Mabuti lang at nagagamit ko ang natututunan ko sa college."

I cracked a small smile.

Stella definitely also knew me well enough not to nag me about it—seeing as I eventually end up telling her everything anyway.

The truth was I had just come from taking an entrance exam to apply for a scholarship at one of the big business schools in Makati.

It was already so intimidating. Even the building where the exam had been set looked so clean and professional. And if I managed to get in, I would be studying among the brightest business students in the entire region.

I knew it was a super long shot and I didn't want to get my hopes up. But in the last few weeks, I had also applied for a scholarship to three other business schools.

No doubt it would be good if someone helped Frank Lloyd with running the business end of things for our band and help us grow.

And if I could get a business degree, I would gain some real-world business knowledge. Or at the very least, you know, I might be able to keep an actually decent job.

I didn't want to tell anyone until I was more confident in my decision but if Martin could finally get up off his ass and fix his life, so should I.

I figured I had nothing to lose and I was going to keep trying until I succeeded.

If you practice excellence every day, you will be excellent by nature.

I couldn't help a shake of my head at the recall. Who knew even some of Tita's venerable wisdom would rub off on me?

The bell on YouTube popped a notification with a ding when a new video appeared on the feed and Jen turned to look. "O, may isa pa."

"Isa pang ano?"

Jen hovered her mouse over several other recommendation preview thumbnails and I narrowed my eyes at the list. "Anong mga 'yan?"

"Ang daming ibang nag-post nung kuha nila ng kanta n'yo," Stella answered. "Sinabi ko nga sa'yo trending eh."

"At sobrang nakakatawa 'yung iba," Jen relayed with a grin as she clicked on the newest clip of our *harana*.

With an astonished smile, I watched the amateurly-captured cellphone video. It started out very shaky with a lot of howling crowd noise overpowering the familiar song.

Jen was already humming along, swaying from side to side in her chair.

"Uyyy! Yihee!" Stella cheered again as the video came to a shot of Ate Roweena's surprised but elated face.

"Aba, may captions ang lolo mo," Jen noted after a moment.

The random internet person uploader had edited the video to include captions and stickers. There were lots of hearts and smileys and sweet words in support of Lance and Ate Roweena.

But then at about 1:58 the view came to a clear shot of me staring intently at something.

I swallowed hard in dread because I clearly remembered exactly where I had been looking at the time. And indeed when the camera panned across quickly, it was to a shot of

Will, standing across the street with a nondescript expression on his face.

Though I imagined it would have been completely innocuous if only the video uploader hadn't decided to caption that moment as well—in big yellow cartoon overlay letters.

Next couple in the making??? Heart heart heart. Kiss. Kiss. Kiss.

A panicked shiver ran up my spine and my eyes nearly popped out again. *Oh my god, WHAT?*

But Stella and Jen burst out laughing.

"Ayan pala naman eh, o Ate Armi. Kung naghahanap ka ng boyfriend, si Will daw." Jen slapped the table repeatedly in her mirth.

Stella shook her head. "Ano ba 'yan? Mga tao talaga, walang magawa. Puro jokes! Diba 'no?" She thumped on my back.

"Baka magunaw muna ang mundo," Jen added.

I chuckled low in my throat, managing not to be offended and riding along to their gag. I heaved a big sigh after a moment. "Or if not, baka naman si Nick may pinsan na pwede mong ma-reto, Stella," I suggested, my tone full of derision.

"Oh my god—"

And the two of them cackled out laughing again.

***

34

Lagot

The electric fans were all on full blast as the typical scorching Philippines summer was rearing its ugly head early.

Sprawled on the floor beside Basti, Martin and Bingka were playing a game on the old iPad. Mom, laundry basket at her hip, was paused near the dining table talking to Dad —probably nitpicking something he'd done while he mostly nodded his head in passive agreement, waiting for her to leave so he could go back to reading the newspaper.

Ate Roweena was sitting on the couch next to me. She kept giggling as she read messages on her phone. No doubt she was talking to Lance.

With my own phone in hand, I stretched out in my seat with a small smile of amusement as I observed my family's default state of being.

When Mom finally peeled away from Dad it was to

approach Ate Roweena. Mom's smile was as big as her face and the likely topic of her discussion with Dad was revealed.

"Rowena, ano sa tingin mo?" Mom prompted. "Siguro naman dapat bongga'ng hotel ang pipiliin natin para sa reception, diba? O baka naman maaaring destination wedding! Sa beach!" Her eyes were bright. "Sa wakas, makakapunta na rin tayo sa Palawan!"

I couldn't help my chuckle.

But Ate Roweena's cheeks flushed red. "Oh my god, Mommy! Hindi pa po kami ikakasal." She tried to wave Mom away.

Mom just laughed self-assuredly. "Hay nako, anak. Trust your mom. I know it will happen." She went on singing to herself as she walked past the living room, coming back in and out several times carrying different laundry baskets. "Ang ganda ganda ng anak ko. Mabuti naman mapapakinabangan sa wakas—"

I shook my head to myself and met Ate Roweena's gaze.

She didn't say anything but I was sure anyone in the immediate vicinity could tell she was absolutely glowing with love and happiness.

I nudged her, teasing. "Yihee. Sila na ulit."

Ate Roweena turned her wide smile to me. She had no comeback. She didn't need a comeback.

I was going to tease her some more but my phone beeped in notification and I glanced down to absently check an email. On impulse, I gasped and grabbed Ate Roweena's arm.

Ate Roweena caught my elated expression as I read the email on my phone. "O, ano 'yan?"

I grinned and held the phone out to her so she could read the screen.

"*Congratulations. You are invited to interview for a slot in our scholarship program—*" Her eyes widened as she grabbed my arm in return, already in a pending triumphant cheer. "What? Armi!"

"Nag-submit ako ng scholarship application sa business school, and apparently, sa awa ng Diyos, pumasa ako sa exam."

Ate Roweena squealed—I had never heard her do that before. She squealed so loud, Bingka jumped in fright for a moment and Basti scrambled up from the floor to run to the gate mistakenly thinking there were visitors or maybe cats.

But Ate Roweena was so happy about her own situation, her delight was easily transferred to everyone else's achievements. She threw her arms around me. "Oh my god, oh my god, oh my god! Congratulations!"

Honestly, I couldn't have been any happier either.

After the last few months of feeling like the biggest loser in the world, it was very reassuring to finally somehow be validated. And if being accepted by a scholarship at a good post-graduate school was anything to go by, I supposed I couldn't be as worthless as I'd initially thought.

I could do anything I wanted. I had always just needed direction. And now, like Martin, I had found mine too.

"Sabi nga ni Frank Lloyd, sa mga panahon ngayon hindi pwedeng isa lang ang diskarte," I relayed.

"Paano 'yung trabaho kina Tito Boy?"

"Hindi na ako nag-renew ng contract."

"Sasabihin mo ba kina Mommy?"

"Oo naman. Lalo na't ngayon sigurado na."

"I'm sure matutuwa si Daddy. At si Mommy..." Ate Roweena paused to consider. "Masasanay din 'yon."

I laughed with her. My chest felt full with happiness. For her. For me. For all of us.

Everything was finally falling into place.

A loud vrooming from outside startled Ate Roweena and the dog again and also me.

I turned sharply to look out the window.

"Ano 'yun?" Dad stood up from his chair, looking in the same direction, still holding his paper.

When the gate clanged open by itself without any of us doing it, I was already sitting up in alarm, but I shot up in my seat when I glimpsed the stiff, regal composure of the person coming through the gate.

Tita's shiny red Benz was parked at our curb. One of her 'henchmen' had opened our gate for her and she had decided to casually march in without waiting for an invitation—because of course, invitations are for peasants.

My jaw had already dropped as I hurried to meet her by the door. "Ah, good afternoon po, Tita." I glanced back to see the rest of my family peeking curiously at us from inside. Mom had poked her head out from the side of the house.

Tita studied my mother up and down with a highly critical look.

My mom had obviously been doing laundry in the backyard. She wiped her wet hands on her apron, astonishment on her face as she gaped at our fancy guest.

I looked back and forth between the two of them awkwardly for a moment before gesturing, "Mommy, this is...Donya Viuda Felicitacion Villareal San Mateo," I recited without taking a breath. "Tita, this is my mom po, Mrs. Adelina Benitez."

Tita didn't respond. She peered at the rest of my gawking family through the window behind me then looked around the small entryway of our gate. "Saan tayo pwedeng mag-usap? Sa garden?"

I assumed her question was directed at me. I blinked. "Um, wala po kami'ng garden."

Tita looked shocked. "Wala kayong garden?"

I gestured towards the back of the house. "Pwede po tayo sa likod bahay."

She sniffed, stuck her nose in the air then moved to walk where I'd directed.

Although after a few steps, it occurred to me that the backyard might not have been the best place to go either as it was littered with my mother's laundry work—the damp clothes hanging on some lines by the back wall.

Tita had to sidestep some puddles, being careful with her most likely designer shoes.

Though at least, the location was private enough.

I wasn't sure what Tita wanted to talk about but the way she was going, I *was* sure my entire family and indeed the entire barangay probably shouldn't be within earshot.

When Tita had settled in her stance, frowning as she moved her head to avoid a laundry mobile hanging by the window, she turned her gaze to me, her directive cold, matter-of-fact.

"I'm sure you already know why I'm here."

I blinked again and had to shake my head after a moment.

Her eyes narrowed like she didn't believe me. "May narinig akong balita," she paused as if in loathing of what she was going to say next. "Na may pagkakaintindihan na daw kayo ng inaanak kong si Will." She huffed haughtily. "Siyempre alam kong malaking kalokohan 'yan dahil sigurado akong imposibleng may anuma'ng koneksyon sa'yo ang inaanak ko."

I wrinkled my nose after a beat. "So...bakit po kayo nandito?"

She stamped her foot—in a puddle, no longer caring about her several-thousand-pesos-worth shoes. "Huwag mo akong lolokohin, iha! Akala mo ba you're the first girl I've seen who wants to take advantage of Will's status in life? I know your type. And it's not going to work."

My jaw had dropped, nearly in indignation, but still mostly confusion. "Um, hindi ko po alam saan n'yo nakuha yung information n'yo pero—"

She cut me off. "Anong hindi mo alam?" she demanded, her eyes flashing. "Paano pa magkakaroon ng chismis na ganyan kung hindi inimbento mo?" She huffed, looking away. "And it's being made worse by that *goddamn* video—which you probably posted yourself to support these ridiculous rumors."

Hala. I gulped in dread, realizing she was referring to that YouTuber's caption of the scene between me and Will that my friends and I had seen the other day.

But OMG. Paano ba naman nakita ni Tita 'yon? I wondered in skepticism. "Um, Tita, hindi ko po talaga kilala 'yung nagpost nu'ng—"

She cut me off again. "I want you to take all those videos down."

I was taken aback, I almost choked. "Po?"

"And I also want you to release a statement for people not to repost the video due to copyright concerns."

"Po?" I repeated in complete aghast.

Aside from the fact that pulling content from the internet was *virtually* impossible, all those videos were giving my band some amazing and much-needed publicity.

Jen was already actively working on making even more videos and promoting our band on social media.

We had all worked so hard for so many years to get this kind of public response. I wasn't about to stifle it just because one random video contained some harmless and blatantly untrue speculation.

"Tita, seriously," I insisted. "Katuwaan lang naman po 'yon siguro nu'ng nag-upload. Desperado lang po magpa-comment para maraming views 'yung video n'ya."

Tita's sharp gaze focused on me again. "Hindi nagsisimula ang mga chismis na ganyan kung walang basehan." One of her eyebrows shot up. "Sabihin mo, totoo ba'ng wala kayo'ng relasyon ng inaanak ko?"

My eyebrows snapped together. I was starting to get irritated by her accusations. "Akala ko po ba sinabi n'yo imposible 'yon?"

That only made her angrier. "Kagatin mo 'yang dila mo, iha! In case walang nag-mention sa'yo, napagkasundo na si Will sa anak kong si Graciella. And by far, di hamak na mas bagay sila, lalo na't sa sitwasyon sa buhay."

I furrowed my eyebrows, even more confused now. "Eh kung ganun naman po pala, paano n'yo pa naisip na may pagkakaintindihan kami ni Will?"

"Aba! Malay ko ba kung ano'ng panunukso ang ginamit mo sa kanya at baka naloko mo na. Baka kinalimutan na ang responsibilidad niya sa pamilya n'ya."

She huffed again. "Akala mo ba tatanggapin ka ng pamilyang Salcedo? Ikaw? Ikaw ang sisira sa mga plano nila? Sisira sa anak nila? Isang babaeng walang ambisyon sa buhay? Anak ng taxi driver at labandera. At 'yung kapatid mo na muntik na'ng makulong?" She nodded emphatically. "Oo, alam ko rin ang tungkol diyan! Magaling lang siguro talaga ang abogado ng puting boyfriend ng tita mo at mabuti may pera. Kung hindi, saan kayo pupulutin?"

I clenched my teeth in fury, her condescending statements stabbing my chest, and I struggled to control the outburst bubbling up my throat.

"Ngayon, sumagot ka ng maayos." She took a deep breath to prepare her next blunt question. "Nililigawan ka ba ng inaanak ko?"

I stiffened for a second before managing to reply, "Hindi po."

She breathed out, her face relaxing considerably. "Good." She gave me a curt nod. "Ngayon...gusto kong marinig galing sa'yo na hindi mo siya tatanggapin maski magtanong siya."

I froze where I stood. It would have been a simple answer '*opo*' and I knew I would have dismissed the matter and *her* away forever but there was a lump in my throat.

And in spite of everything, I knew in my heart my real answer was, "No."

"No?" Tita looked gobsmacked—ironically, looking much the same way as Will had when I had turned him down at the mall the first time. It was almost alarming to recognize how similar their personalities, in fact, were.

My chest constricted again. Because if Tita looked down on me this way, how could Will possibly not? How could Will possibly see me in any other way except for exactly how Tita had just described?

A no-ambition girl from a poor, embarrassing family. What fraction of hope could I actually even really have with him? And if he already had doubts about the feasibility of us beforehand, given the influence Tita's advice had on all her family, that small fraction probably quickly reduced to zero.

Tita was still staring at me. "Nasisiraan ka na ba ng bait, iha?"

I bit my lip. *Posible.*

Somewhat fortunately though, Tita had caught me at my most confident time ever. She and Will might think I was a worthless girl with no ambition but I had hard proof to the contrary. And my family, in spite of our lack of wealth, had more integrity and care than Tita was showing right then.

I was not going to be bullied by her.

I took a deep breath myself before starting, "Hindi po ako nasisiraan ng bait at wala po akong ginagawang masama. Malaya po akong magpaligaw kung kanino ko gusto. And just because mayaman po kayo, it doesn't mean pwede kayong makialam sa buhay ng iba. Hindi po namin kayo kaano-ano. At kung nagpunta po kayo dito para lang mang-insulto, I think max na po so pwede na po kayong umalis." I gave her a little dismissive wave.

Tita's jaw dropped so low I could almost see her tonsils.

When she didn't move, I motioned my little wave again and gave her a prompting look to go away.

Tita's eyes bulged and her face turned red before she whirled around in a flurry of dogwood *eau de parfum* and Surf laundry powder as she brushed past some more laundry to stomp away.

I followed suit and watched Tita march back out through our gate—mostly to make sure she actually left. I watched as she got into her car and waited for it to drive away before I finally heaved a sigh of relief, collapsing against the wall.

I jumped when my phone went off again. I was already frowning with the preview, a message from Stella, before I swiped to read the whole thing.

OMG. I'm sorry. I'm sorry. Nadulas ako ng kwento kay Nick about Will in that video. And he told Tita. She freaked out and I think she's on her way to see you. I'M SO SO SO SO SO SORRY!!!

I grimaced. Well-meaning as it was, Stella's text warning had come just a bit too late.

I blew out another big, deep sigh, trying to shake off the entire horrible encounter before turning back to return to the house.

Bingka watched me come in. "Sino po 'yon, Ate?"

I took a moment to assign a smile back onto my face. "A, wala, nagkamali lang," I dismissed.

Ate Roweena glanced up from her seat on the couch to catch my gaze with a *yeah-right* look but she simply went back to texting Lance.

"Carmina!" Mom cried out.

Almost on the verge of panic at her tone, I looked over

and found Mom in the kitchen with her mouth hanging open as she held up several condiment bottles—all of which carried the Tita Fely branding and logo with Tita's actual face on it.

"Ito 'yung babae!"

I just laughed out loud.

35

Benta

I couldn't remember the last time I had woken up so early on a Sunday. I got dressed as quietly as I could, making sure not to wake up Ate Roweena, and moved through the seeming deserted house like I would have done if I was sneaking back in after a long night out with friends without permission.

Admittedly, it felt odd to be suddenly filled with purpose. The next chapter of my life was beginning and maybe I just couldn't wait to start it.

I was going to Makati to submit some paperwork for my scholarship application. I didn't need to be there until mid-morning but I wanted to beat the rush hour traffic commute. I didn't want anything to stress me out today.

I had worn my only block-heeled pair of shoes and business casual pants, my blazer jacket hung on my arm. I was planning to play the part of an MBA-scholarship hopeful to perfection.

My parents' reaction to my new direction in life was certainly as expected. Dad was happy for me. Mom was a bit apprehensive about me giving up the stable job at Tito Boy's and even more skeptical about my 'fancy MBA ambitions' but I was sure she was going to get used to the idea.

Anyway, Mom was much enthusiastically, if prematurely, preoccupied with all the pipe dream details for the imminent wedding of her favorite daughter.

And if I could brush off my mother's everlasting dis-appointment in me, one could just imagine how Tita's scandalous insults from yesterday were merely water off the duck's back.

My nosy family didn't think much about Tita's random visit for a change and I definitely wasn't eager to volunteer more information about it.

The whole incident was passed off and had faded into the early morning South Manila mist, as with the sunrise hidden behind the clouds, the whole park area in front of our house was ghostly gray and empty.

I also realized there wasn't much I could do with the whole Tita/Will issue anyway. That was, if Tita's directive to Will meant that he would never see me again then that was how it was going to be.

Despite the achy, heavy feeling in my chest, I was sure I would eventually get over that too. He was just some guy anyway...

I pushed through our gate, wincing as its rusty hinges squeaked as if to announce my exit.

I thought I saw the figure of some guy sitting at the other

side of the chapel steps across the street and I narrowed my eyes to try to make out his form.

He'd had his back to me and spun around upon hearing the gate squeak and my eyes nearly popped out of my head when I recognized his face.

His own eyes lit up when he met my gaze and he quickly straightened up.

Will was wearing stonewashed jeans and a manga-print T-shirt. The most casual look I had ever seen on him.

Dayummm. Bakit ang pogi pa rin?

My heart started to pound in my chest when he strode across the chapel walkway headed towards our side of the street.

I snapped to attention and walked up to meet him halfway, stopping at the chapel threshold as he arrived. I was entirely too baffled to say anything first. It was as if the entire morning needed to shift around me to accommodate his unexpected presence.

Will's forehead was already creased as he regarded my quizzical expression. "Are you okay?"

Was I okay? Good question.

He went on when I didn't respond. "I don't even want to imagine anong sinabi sa'yo ni Ninang kahapon." He shook his head in distress, in indignation, before he leveled his gaze with mine again. "I am so sorry."

I blinked in incredulity. *He* was sorry? Stopping my jaw from dropping, I fired out, "Sira ulo ka ba?"

He jumped at my sharp response. "What?"

I whacked the side of his arm twice in frustration. "Matapos lahat ng ginawa mo—ikaw ang sorry?"

Will gave me a ridiculous look before rubbing his arm pointedly. "Ouch."

I blew out a breath, the tension dissipating from my shoulders, and I met his gaze again, more calmly this time. "Ako dapat ang mag-sorry," I declared. "Paano ba kami makakapag-pasalamat sa'yo sa lahat ng ginawa mo para kay Martin? Para kay Ate?"

When he finally stopped looking wary that I was going to hit him again, the corner of Will's mouth turned up into the most mesmerizing shy smile I had ever seen.

"Para sa'yo."

A shiver ran up my neck at the rumble in his voice.

He dropped his gaze for a moment. "There's no excuse for Ninang's behavior. Pero thanks to her, for once, bumalik ang pag-asa ko." He cracked a quirky smile. "Ayaw mo daw umatras," he relayed, sounding impressed. "So I thought maybe—"

But his face fell again, almost already in desolation. "I mean, I'll understand completely if you tell me to leave you alone, if you were just being nice."

He sighed again before his imploring eyes returned to mine. "But I'm hoping...nagbago na ang isip mo sa'kin because...I still really like you."

I bit my lip, already brimming with hope and anticipation. I almost couldn't contain it.

OMG—like where do I even start?

I took a moment to pull myself together, swallowing hard before I took a brave step closer. I laid my hand on his chest, unable to help my smile as I noticed, "Your heart is beating so fast."

"It's yours."

I stared up into his face, the first streaks of the sunrise peeking through the clouds making his eyes sparkle as he gazed down at me. I took a deep breath in reassurance, in contentment. "Good."

Will lifted his hand to touch my cheek and when I didn't resist, his own smile widened. He leaned his forehead against mine, breathing deeply, his eyes closing for a second. "Good."

After a long wonderful minute, he pulled away, his eyebrows furrowing. "Tumangkad ka ba?"

I scrunched my face up at him. "Salamat ha. I'm wearing heels." I gestured down to my feet.

Will tilted his head to one side to give my outfit a look up and down. "Anong lakad mo today?"

"Ah, I've been applying for scholarships sa business schools. May kailangan lang akong asikasuhin na papels today."

Will's eyes lit up again in what I thought was surprise until he shook his head again. "What a funny coincidence," he remarked, averting his gaze. "Hey, when is your appointment? Do you have time right now?"

"Bakit?" I was trying to guess the reason for his mysterious expression.

"I want to show you something."

I should have recognized the street where we were. I should have recognized the shops we were driving past. But I couldn't stop staring at Will's profile as he drove. The last time I was in his car, I had wanted to kill him.

I was sure my face was super red but I couldn't help it.

"I can't drive with you staring at me like that," Will chided even as he had a stupid smile on too.

I chuckled and finally turned my head to look out the window as the car rolled to a stop at the curb.

I recognized the place instantly.

It was the bar my band used to play at. The one that had closed last year. The windows were still boarded up, the decorative vines around the trellis were overgrown, and the neon signage had been removed.

But there was a new notice hanging on the door. One that read 'Under New Management.'

I turned back to Will with my mouth already hanging open in astonishment as everything clicked in my head. "Binili mo 'yung bar?" It was more a statement than a question.

Will shrugged. "I thought it was a good investment," he replied and grinned again. "And now maybe I'll have a future business partner."

My jaw was on the floor. I couldn't speak. In awe. In gratitude.

As if it wasn't enough, he added, "It would also mean you get to choose which bands get to play."

I could have cried.

"Consider this an apology for one of the first things you heard me say."

He looked so guilty. It was so adorable.

"I still can't forget when you said there was absolutely no way you were ever going to like me. *Ever.*"

I groaned, grimacing. "Oh my god, 'wag mo na ulitin. I was such a bitch."

"But you were right," he pointed out. "I was so mayabang. I needed to step off my pedestal."

"Well, actually ako rin," I had to admit. "I pre-judged you. Puro kasi unverified chismis."

"I guess we make each other better." He smiled before pausing as if to add an afterthought, "Well, I mean, not that *I* needed much improvement."

And I shot him an incredulous look with my mirth. "Hay nako! Alam mo, ang yabang mo pa rin."

He laughed. "Okay lang." A shadow of a smirk hung around his mouth. "Astig ka naman, diba?"

I rolled my eyes, scoffing, "Halikan kita diyan eh."

His eyes lit up. "Promise?"

36

Epilogue

"Hala, ayan na." Mom elbowed my dad who was trying to snooze in his chair beside her. "Narinig mo ba, Rene? Una, may pag-e-MBA na nalalaman. Tapos ayan, mag-bi-business daw."

Even with all the giant electric fans blowing in every corner, Bingka's school's gym was still stifling hot.

"Mabuti hindi naman nagalit si Boy. Sayang din 'yung trabaho. Paano ngayon, mag-aantay muna tayo sa mga part time jobs na 'yan hangga't matapos ang pag-aaral ulit? Hmph."

Maybe Mom was just trying to keep from getting bored from watching the four-hour graduation ceremony.

I certainly needed all the help I could get. I slumped back to get as comfortable as I could be in my foldable metal seat, my phone in my hand as we all waited for Bingka's turn to be called to come up the stage.

We were near the middle of the handful of rows of chairs of about a hundred people looking just as bored with the proceedings, some in the same state as my dad but the majority of them on their cellphones.

I glanced over at Ate Roweena and Lance sitting on the other side of my parents'. The two lovebirds' heads were leaned towards each other as they played some kind of train game on Lance's phone.

Did I mention they had barely spent an hour apart since Valentine's Day? I smiled as I took in my sister's expression as she playfully tapped Lance's arm. I had never seen her so open and happy ever before. I had such high hopes for the two of them.

Martin was in the seat further up. He was in his default setting—bent over his own phone, playing a cyberpunk game, his earphones plugged in, completely in his own world. Mr. Future Lawyer.

A smattering of applause took my attention back to the stage as the school's valedictorian finished with her speech.

Mom went on and on like a sermon. "Mag-bi-business daw with William Salcedo, 'yung mayabang. Naalala mo ba 'yon? Ay, nasisiraan na talaga ng bait ang anak mo."

I was hoping the other people seated around us didn't mind her rambling. Lance for sure was too preoccupied with Ate Roweena to mind my mom's disparaging remarks about his best friend.

Meanwhile, Dad had drifted off, starting to snore—which made him jump up and wake again.

"Hoy, Rene. Narinig mo ba 'yung sinabi ko? Hindi ba

napaka-yabang nu'ng taong 'yun?" Mom snapped her prompt. "Siguradong walang mararating na mabuti 'yan. Pagsasabihan mo ba 'yang paborito mong anak?"

"Gusto mo ba pagsabihan ko siya?" Dad responded. "O, Armi, anak. Sabi ng nanay mo 'wag ka daw makipag-business diyan sa mayabang na William Salcedo."

I bit back my smile. "Hindi naman siya ganun ka-yabang," I spoke up.

Mom narrowed her eyes at me. "Halaaa, ayan na! May sakit ka ba, Carmina?"

My phone buzzed and I glanced down to read the message, instantly smiling.

I'm here.

I moved to get up.

"O, saan ka pupunta? Baka malapit na tawagin ang class ni Bingka," Mom started, her eyebrows up on her forehead like she didn't want me to miss a moment of her complaints.

"Diyan lang po sa likod," I replied in a hoarse whisper, not giving my mom an opportunity to respond before I walked away.

Will was standing a few feet behind the back rows, his hands in the pockets of his pants. He had gone back to wearing his usual business casual clothes, his button-down shirt sleeves rolled up his arms, his hair impeccable as always.

The smile on his face was new.

I beamed at him as I approached.

"I thought hindi ka makakapunta today?" I asked in a hushed tone.

Will craned his neck and I turned to notice my mom's

suspicious stare back at us. I could imagine my mom probably thought she conjured the devil just by mentioning his name so many times.

But Will's tone was wry. "Your family still hates me, don't they?"

I huffed. "Care ko ba."

"Good, 'cause I don't care either."

"Sabihin ko ba 'yung tungkol kay Martin?" I suggested, peering up at him. "Sasambahin ka ng nanay ko."

He groaned. "Daldal talaga ng kapatid mong 'yan."

"Pasalamat ka kamo't nadulas siya," I reminded him.

"Hmp. Pasalamat ka daw."

I felt Will take my hand in his and I glanced down, almost in surprise, and the entire length of my arm tingled in happiness and pleasure.

But I just bit my lip and focused my attention back to the stage of the graduation ceremony. Not looking at him. Not saying anything.

I only heard Will's soft chuckle as he stood beside me, not saying anything either.

Nothing further needed to be said.

Ate Roweena happened to turn back towards us and her eyes lit up with delighted awe. She tugged on Lance's arm to turn around to look.

Lance just grinned, as surely, he must have already known.

Martin glanced over his shoulder for the briefest of moments to see what was up but then dropped his gaze back to his game, zero cares given.

Meanwhile, Mom's jaw was close to being unhinged in

shock. She was so eager to wake Dad up from his snoring to have a look, she elbowed him too hard and Dad fell off his chair with a loud crash.

The End

About the Author

ZARA IRIGO hails from Las Pinas City, Metro Manila. She grew up in the nineties when everything was just a shade better. She writes contemporary and fantasy fiction in her default language – Taglish.

Her first book, a contemporary chick-lit romance "Five Days in Palawan" was published in 2007. Sign up to her mailing list to hear about book news. **https://bit.ly/keepintouchwithzara**

Follow her on Facebook
www.facebook.com/fivedaysinpalawan

Follow her on Instagram
www.instagram.com/fivedaysinpalawan

Other books by Zara Irigo

Okay, Life.

Set in the early 2000's - the days before social networking, the era of the mallrats, when people still used pay phones and landlines, texting was only on the rise, and NU 107 was still on the air.

Lia Alvarez, an 18-year old student, takes up 'the antipatiko challenge' when her fate collides (literally) with Jeffrey Gutierrez, the hottest guy ever with a hidden backstory.

A love story, but mostly a life story. A tribute - to the 90's kids. *This book is FREE for mailing list subscribers.*

Ghosts of Unfinished Stories Past

What if nahanap mo na yung soulmate mo? Pero fictional character pala siya. What's more, ikaw pala ang nag-imbento sa kanya. Sa dinami-dami ng kwentong nasulat mo, sa dinami-dami ng mundong na-imbento mo, saan kayo magtatagpo? Magkakatuluyan ba kayo sa wakas?

Lea Ignacio takes the phrase "getting lost in your books" to a whole new level. Then again, as the saying goes, reading is an escape from reality. But what if...you couldn't escape from your escape...? *Coming soon.*

Limang Araw sa Palawan

"Limang Araw sa Palawan" is the 10th anniversary version

of "Five Days in Palawan" - a Filipino novel. This exclusive edition is available for purchase for a limited time. Visit **https://www.subscribepage.com/zarairigoauthor** for more details.